THE BOBBSEY TWINS
IN ESKIMO LAND

Heather from Nannie
July 6th 1960.

. . . a perfect landing on the broad icefield . . .

The Bobbsey Twins in Eskimo Land

By
LAURA LEE HOPE

Published by
WORLD DISTRIBUTORS (MANCHESTER) LIMITED
LONDON – MANCHESTER
ENGLAND

THE BOBBSEY TWINS BOOKS

By Laura Lee Hope

THE BOBBSEY TWINS
THE BOBBSEY TWINS AT SCHOOL
THE BOBBSEY TWINS IN THE COUNTRY
THE BOBBSEY TWINS AT MEADOW BROOK
THE BOBBSEY TWINS AT THE SEASHORE
THE BOBBSEY TWINS ON A HOUSEBOAT
THE BOBBSEY TWINS CAMPING OUT
THE BOBBSEY TWINS ON BLUEBERRY ISLAND
THE BOBBSEY TWINS AT SNOW LODGE
THE BOBBSEY TWINS' WONDERFUL SECRET
THE BOBBSEY TWINS AT THE CIRCUS
THE BOBBSEY TWINS SOLVE A MYSTERY
THE BOBBSEY TWINS AT WHITESAIL HARBOUR
THE BOBBSEY TWINS AT MYSTERY MANSION
THE BOBBSEY TWINS IN RAINBOW VALLEY
THE BOBBSEY TWINS AND THE HORSESHOE RIDDLE
THE BOBBSEY TWINS AT BIG BEAR POND
THE BOBBSEY TWINS ON A BICYCLE TRIP
THE BOBBSEY TWINS TREASURE HUNTING
THE BOBBSEY TWINS AT SUGAR MAPLE HILL
THE BOBBSEY TWINS IN ESKIMO LAND
THE BOBBSEY TWINS AT LIGHTHOUSE POINT
THE BOBBSEY TWINS IN ECHO VALLEY
THE BOBBSEY TWINS ON THE PONY TRAIL

CONTENTS

CHAPTER I

THE IGLOO

"WHY, Flossie, that's *good*! It really is a pretty picture."

Nan Bobbsey was looking at a large drawing of an Eskimo igloo which her little sister had made in school that day. It was a very good likeness of a big snow-house with windows of ice.

Freddie stood by, staring at what his twin had made. Suddenly he gave a jump and said, "That gives me an idea." Then he ran out of the room and up the stairs as fast as he could.

"You do like the picture, don't you, Nan?" Flossie asked eagerly.

"Very much."

Nan bent over the dining-room table on which the drawing had been put. The little girl stood close to her elder sister, and traced an outline of the igloo with a fat finger.

"It makes you feel cold just to look at it," Nan continued. "And the snow seems real, Flossie."

"As if you could walk right into the place and start making a snowman," said Flossie. "Anyway, that's what Freddie said."

"What yo' all got there?"

7

Black Dinah, the jolly old cook of the Bobbsey family, came in from the kitchen just then with a plate of home-made cookies in her hand.

"Sho' do look cold," she said, to the little girl's delight. "All dat ice an' snow look like wintah, an' no mistake. An' what's dis here thing?" she asked, pointing to the igloo. "One ob dem iggles Ah hears tell about?"

Flossie chuckled, and even Nan had to laugh.

"Not iggle, Dinah—igloo," the taller girl corrected. "That's the kind of house some Eskimos live in. They're made of blocks of ice, and the people keep nice and warm inside."

"And the Eskimos eat a lot of fat to help them keep from freezing," added Flossie, eager to show how much she had learned.

"Well, all Ah has to say is dat folks as lives in snowhouses got to eat somepin' to keep their bones fum turnin' into ice cycles, yes ma'am," said Dinah with a shiver. "Ah don't like de idea ob dat, nohow."

"I'd love to live in one," said Flossie with an excited bounce. "And so would Freddie. He said so."

"Yo' all would be lucky ef yo' didn't freeze yo'-selves to death," said Dinah. "S'pose some day yo' all turns into two little white ice cycles. How yo' all goin' like dat?"

"I wouldn't like it," said Flossie. "Whoever heard of icicles having any fun? Do you know what kind of a picture Freddie drew?" she added.

"No. What?" asked Nan.

"Anudder ob dem eeg-glues?" asked Dinah, getting ready to leave.

"A fur trapper. It is pretty good, but Teacher liked mine better——"

Bump! Bump! Bump!

A great thudding somewhere in the front part of the house made Nan rush into the hall with Dinah and Flossie close behind her. There they found what at first seemed to be a great round mass of fur. From this fuzzy ball there came grunts and gasps, then a muffled cry from little Freddie Bobbsey.

Nan ran forward and grasped the bundle of fluff by what looked to be the top of it. She pulled, and presently her little brother came out, looking very red and mussed up. He was just the least bit ashamed, it seemed.

"Golly," said the small boy, "I didn't mean to, honest, Nan. I just put on Mother's fur coat to find out how it would feel to be a fur trapper, and I—I tripped and—and fell down the stairs."

"I hope you haven't spoiled the coat," said Nan.

"Oh, look!" Flossie pointed to a long, jagged rip in the beautiful fur. "It's all torn. What will Mother say?"

"My!" said Freddie. "I didn't mean to tear it. I'm awfully sorry."

"What's that you have in your hand?" Bert Bobbsey, Nan's twin, drawn from another part of the house by all the noise, pointed to a fishing-rod Freddie was holding. "Isn't that Dad's pole?"

"Y-yes," said Freddie. "I was playing trapper, you see, and I thought I might catch some fish."

"And instead you fell downstairs and spoiled a good fur coat," said Nan, trying to speak very firmly. "I don't know what Mother will say when she sees it."

"Maybe we can get it fixed," Bert suggested "Mr. Palant, the man who has the fur store, would mend it, I guess."

"Oh, let's go there," said Flossie eagerly. "He has so many fuzzy little animals in his store. I like to look at them."

The two sets of Bobbsey twins left for the furrier's shop, carrying their mother's wrap. As they went out the door, Freddie said loudly:

"Anyway, I still think I want to be an Eskimo. And Daddy may have to play he's one too if he goes up North, the way he said he might."

Dinah, closing the door, mumbled something the children could not hear, but which would have surprised them greatly.

"And ef what I heerd Mr. Bobbsey say, come true, den yo' all gwine be playing Eskimo, too!"

At the furrier's the children found Mr. Palant quite willing to repair Mrs. Bobbsey's coat. He assured them that the damage was slight and could be mended easily.

Freddie sighed deeply. "I'm so glad," he said. "I thought I had spoiled it."

Mr. Palant took the children through his shop, letting them examine his many stuffed animals, and giving his visitors a little talk on the habits of live ones like them.

Finally, Flossie stopped before a small beaver covered with glossy brown fur. The little girl clapped her hands in delight.

"Oh, how pretty!" she cried. "I wish I could take it home with me."

"It *is* pretty," agreed Mr. Palant. "And this animal

isn't at all like the others you have seen. It can talk," he added with a laugh.

"Oh," cried Flossie. "Is it alive?"

Mr. Palant did not answer, but walked around until he was behind the counter. What he did the children did not know, but suddenly the beaver gave a sharp squeak and moved forward. Flossie ran behind Nan, and even Freddie stepped back so suddenly that he bumped into Bert.

"It *is* alive!" gasped Flossie. "Oh, please, Mr. Palant, take it away!"

The man laughed and came out from behind the counter.

"It isn't alive," he said. "The stand it is on squeaks, that's all. The beaver is not fastened on tightly, so in that way it can be pushed forward an inch or two. That makes it look as if it really moved."

"I knew all the time it wasn't alive," said little Freddie, and the others smiled.

The store was such a wonderful place the children could not bear to leave it. They were just about to decide that they really should go, when Mr. Palant remarked that he was planning to change his show window, but was not sure just how he might go about it.

"Not very many people have come to my shop lately," he said sadly. "I ought to fix up my window so men and women in the street will notice it and maybe come in."

Flossie had a great idea at this moment. "Wouldn't it be pretty to make an Eskimo scene in the store window, and use some of your nice furry animals and—and maybe an igloo, the kind of house the people live in way up North?"

"You have the picture you made in school right in your hand," said Bert. "Maybe we can use it."

Flossie saw that what Bert had said was right, and that she really had brought her drawing all the way from home without knowing it.

"I must have picked it up from the table. I put it there when I heard Freddie fall down the stairs," she said. "Mr. Palant, do you think we could use this?"

The furrier put on his spectacles and held the picture up to the light.

"Very pretty, very good indeed," he said. "I think we might use this as part of our background."

"And have this baby seal in the front," Nan suggested, warming to the idea.

"I have a big picture of a trapper in my bureau drawer," Freddie said. "Maybe we could use that, too."

"Go over to the house and get it," cried Bert. "That will look just right on the other side of the show window."

The little boy ran home as fast as his feet could carry him. In the meantime, the other children got busy and helped Mr. Palant. A wolf with a beautiful glossy coat, an Arctic fox, and finally a white polar bear were set in the window. Very attractive the scene looked, especially when Freddie's picture of the trapper was set up where everyone could see it.

"Oh, that's nice!" cried Flossie. "And look, Mr. Palant, people are beginning to stop before the window already!"

CHAPTER II

A LOST PURSE

IT was true that the window had already begun to attract attention. Two women with a little boy between them stopped to admire it. From within the shop the Bobbseys heard the child say, "Oh, look, Mama—what pretty pictures!"

Other people paused to gaze at them, too, and Mr. Palant seemed to be very much pleased.

"I believe it will be a success," he said to the children. "I shall have to give you something for every extra sale I make."

Nan and Bert smiled at this, but Freddie and Flossie were too excited to notice what he said.

"There's a lady coming into the shop," cried the little boy. "Golly! I hope she wants to buy something."

She was young and very nice looking, but seemed a little surprised when she saw four pair of eyes looking at her so closely. She turned to Mr. Palant and smiled.

"Your show window is very attractive," she said. "I heard several people admiring it as I came in."

"You will have to hold these young folks responsible, Miss Lamson," said Mr. Palant, pointing to the two sets of Bobbsey twins. "They did it all."

"Really! Well, I think that's very clever," said Miss Lamson. "The pictures are so cold-looking that they make one want to buy furs to keep warm. Did you children draw them?"

"Flossie drew the igloo and I made the trapper," said Freddie. "Flossie draws better than I do, though," he added.

"We-ell, I don't know about that," said Miss Lamson. "I like the trapper very much, too. You know, those pictures make me feel just a little bit homesick. I come from way up North."

"Honest?" cried Freddie. "Way up North?"

"Way up North," nodded Miss Lamson. "From a place called Cold Star on Hudson Bay."

"Oh, tell us about it!" cried Freddie. "Isn't it awfully cold there?"

While Mr. Palant was getting a fur scarf Miss Lamson had left with him to be repaired, the young lady spoke of her work as a teacher in the settlement at Cold Star. She described the place as though she loved it. Her eager listeners, seeing it through her eyes, felt that they wanted to go there, too.

"I wish we could take a trip up North," said Freddie. "That would be swell."

"Maybe we can," Flossie said hopefully, "if Daddy goes there on business."

"I wouldn't count on that," Bert cautioned. "He may not go, you know."

"And if he does he probably won't want to take all of us along," Nan added.

At this point Mr. Palant came back with Miss Lamson's fur scarf. The teacher said it looked very nice, and turned to reach for her purse. A strange look came over her face as she did so.

"Why, I can't find it," she said. "It's gone!"

"If you had it when you came into the store it must still be here, Miss Lamson," said Mr. Palant kindly. "We will just look about a little and perhaps find it."

"Maybe it fell on the floor," said Nan.

Though the children searched the shop thoroughly, looking behind counters, under chairs, and in every possible corner, nowhere could they see the missing purse.

"I can't understand it," said Miss Lamson unhappily. "I am sure I had my purse with me when I left the restaurant a short time ago."

"But are you certain you had it when you came in here?" asked Mr. Palant.

"No, I'm not." Miss Lamson looked about her helplessly. "Now that I come to think of it, I can't remember having it after I paid my bill at the restaurant where I had tea."

"Was there much money in the purse?" asked Nan.

"A good deal," said Miss Lamson unhappily. "I had some jewellery, too, that I valued highly."

"Maybe you dropped your bag on the street on your way over here," Bert suggested. "We can help you to look."

"Oh, will you?" the lady said gratefully. "I really am dreadfully worried. I must find my purse."

They all went into the street except Mr. Palant, who promised to hold Miss Lamson's fur for her until she was ready to call for it.

"Now we will follow my route from the restaurant as closely as we can," said Miss Lamson. "You children keep your eyes wide open. If you find my purse, I promise you a really nice reward."

"Oh, we wouldn't want you to give us anything," said Flossie, quite shocked at the idea.

"Mother and Daddy wouldn't let us take anything for helping you," added Freddie.

"Thank you just the same," added Nan, who was very thoughtful of other people.

Miss Lamson carefully retraced her steps to the restaurant, while the children kept a sharp look-out for the lost purse.

Once Freddie was sure he saw it. "There it is!" he shouted, and almost bumped into two old ladies who had to pull up sharply to let him pass. "I see it!"

But when Freddie reached the object he was so certain was the purse, he found only a crumpled brown kid glove, much trampled and scuffed by the feet of passers-by.

"Never mind," said Miss Lamson, noting the look of disappointment on Freddie's face. "A kid glove does look something like a purse at a distance. We'll find it yet."

"Are there any other places to look?" asked Nan.

"Ye-es," said Miss Lamson thoughtfully. "I stopped in front of two or three windows on a couple of these side streets. We might go there."

Up and down went the little procession. The children kept a sharp look-out, pausing to examine anything that in any way looked like a lady's handbag. Twice they thought they had it, but each time the "purse" turned out to be something entirely different. One was nothing but a ball of brown paper; another turned out to be the cover of an old school book which some child had thrown carelessly into a gutter.

They were all feeling rather discouraged when Miss Lamson suggested that they inquire for the lost article in the restaurant where she had tea. "If it isn't there," she said, worried, "I am sure I will not know where to look."

The eating-place was only a block or two away, and the little group hurried towards it. When they got there, the young lady went over to the desk and told her story. The clerk was very polite, but she was quite certain that no purse had been turned in that day.

"I'm sorry. The contents of the purse were very valuable," said Miss Lamson. She started to move away, and then added, "You won't mind if we look around a little near the table where I had my tea?"

"Not at all," said the clerk. "I will send one of our girls to help you."

Miss Lamson's table was near the back of the restaurant. She led the way over there at once, the children following close behind her.

There were only a few people left in the place and the tables in the rear were for the most part vacant. Miss Lamson easily found the right one and pointed it out to the Bobbseys.

"I sat there," she said, indicating a chair, "and my purse was at my elbow while I was having tea."

"Did you pay your check here at the table?" asked the waitress, who had been sent to help in the search.

"I think so; yes, I am sure I did." Miss Lamson looked even more worried. "But if I had been so careless as to have left my purse behind me, it should still be here in the restaurant."

"Perhaps some dishonest person saw it and picked it up," added the waitress.

"Or it might have fallen to the floor," said Nan. "Let's look under all the tables and chairs. Perhaps it's hidden away in a corner somewhere."

The children scattered to search the place thoroughly, though to be absolutely truthful they had little hope left of finding the leather bag. They could not help but feel that the waitress was right, and that if Miss Lamson had left her purse in the eating-place some dishonest person had seen it and made off with it.

They were about to give up looking for it, when little Freddie came out from behind an umbrella stand with something clutched tightly in his chubby fist.

"I've found it!" he cried. "And this time it really is a purse."

While Freddie is enjoying his discovery, I shall take just a moment to introduce the Bobbsey twins to those of my readers who do not already know them. There are two sets—Nan and Bert, the brown-eyed older pair; and Freddie and Flossie, blue-eyed and mischievous.

The Bobbsey family, including Father and Mother and the four children, live in the small town of Lakeport, where Mr. Bobbsey is in the lumber business.

Black Dinah is their jolly, fat cook. Her husband, Sam Johnson, works in the garden and sometimes drives the family car.

The first adventures of our little friends are told in the book called "The Bobbsey Twins". In the story just before the one you are now reading, and named "The Bobbsey Twins At Lighthouse Point", the children had many interesting adventures.

And now let us return to Freddie Bobbsey as he ran towards Miss Lamson, the purse he had found clutched tightly in his hand. The young lady cried out with joy as the little boy proudly held it towards her.

"It *is* mine," she said happily. "I can't tell you how glad I am to get it. If only——" She broke off suddenly and stared at it. "Why, there's nothing in it! The money is gone—and so are the jewels. All that is left is a timetable and a key!"

At first the children thought Miss Lamson must be mistaken. Even after she had handed the purse to them and they had turned out its contents on the table top, they still felt that the money and jewels must be hidden somewhere inside. However, all they could find was one dime which had been caught in a fold of the lining.

"No use looking any further," said Miss Lamson. She shut the purse and turned to the door. "I will leave my name and address here. If the money and jewels should turn up, the owners will let me know. That's about all I can do."

She paused a moment at the desk, then went out into the street. Miss Lamson was just going to say good-bye to her young friends, when Mr. Bobbsey came up to them and said to his children:

"Well, aren't you a long way from home? What are you doing here?"

"Miss Lamson, this is our father," said Nan, making the introduction in her best grown-up style. "Maybe Dad can help you find your money," she added. "Dad is good at finding things."

While the grown folks, helped out by Nan, were talking about the kind lady's loss, Freddie tugged at Bert's sleeve.

"Look at that police dog," he said. "He's been sniffing around with his nose to the ground for ever so long. I'll bet he's going to find something."

"Maybe," Bert replied, not paying much attention.

Freddie tugged at his brother's sleeve again.

"It has found something, Bert. Golly, it has something in its mouth. Maybe——"

"We'd better find out what it is!"

CHAPTER III

THE JEWEL BAG

MR. BOBBSEY was listening kindly to the story of Miss Lamson's loss, and how she and the twins had tried to get back the money and the jewels. He promised to help in whatever way he could.

In the course of conversation, Mr. Bobbsey learned that Miss Lamson was one of a number of settlement workers from the Hudson Bay district, and his interest in what the young teacher told him increased.

"I dare say you are well acquainted with that part of the world," he said.

"Oh, very well," smiled Miss Lamson. "I have worked at the settlement for several years, and know most of the people who come and go. As for the natives—I sometimes think I am closer to them than I am to my own people. When I come home here on a visit it takes me some time to get used to conditions."

"She knows a lot of Eskimos, Daddy," said Flossie excitedly. "Real live Eskimos!"

"And so will I," laughed Mr. Bobbsey, "if I follow out my present plans and go to Hudson Bay."

"Golly! Are you really going, Daddy?" asked Freddie.

"I may," said his father. "I want to locate a man

named Weller, a Mr. Harry Weller. I must find him before a certain time. I wonder," with an inquiring look at Miss Lamson, "if you have ever heard of him?"

"I think not," said Miss Lamson slowly. "Although the name has a familiar sound——"

"Will you take us with you, Daddy?" Flossie was so excited she forgot to be polite. "And if we go, may we live in an igloo, the way the Eskimos do?"

"Whoa there, not so fast!" Mr. Bobbsey said, laughing. "Nothing is certain about this Northern trip."

"But if you go, you will take us along, won't you, Daddy?" Nan pleaded.

"Well, well, we'll see," said Mr. Bobbsey. "I can't promise anything just now. Hallo," he added, looking about him, "where do you suppose Bert and Freddie could have gone?"

"I think they ran off after a police dog," Miss Lamson said. "They dashed through the crowd at the end of the street and disappeared around the corner."

"Oh, I wish I had seen them," cried Flossie. "I should have gone with them."

"You are better off right here," said Nan, and clasped her little sister's hand very tightly.

Meanwhile, Bert and Freddie were having their own adventures. Seeing that his father was busy talking, Freddie had pulled at his brother's sleeve.

"Look at that police dog," the little boy had said. "He's been sniffing around with his nose to the ground for ever so long. I'll bet he's going to find something."

"Maybe," Bert had replied, not much interested.

Then Freddie had tugged at his brother's sleeve again. "It has found something, Bert. Golly, it has something in its mouth. Maybe——"

"We'd better find out what it is," Bert had said.

Both boys had gone over to the dog, very quietly at first, then more quickly, as the animal began moving away from them.

"What's he got?" said Freddie excitedly. "Do you s'pose it's a bone?"

"Looks like anything but a bone to me," said Bert. "Watch out! There he goes!"

The dog suddenly broke into a run, darted through the crowd, and made for the street corner with Bert and Freddie after him. Around the corner they went at a great rate, the dog dashing in and out between the legs of people.

As the boys swung out so as not to run down an old man in front of them, they bumped into a mean-looking fellow who seemed to be hurrying in the same direction as they were. The man staggered, and almost fell into the gutter.

"Watch out, can't you!" he growled. "I've a good mind to teach you some manners, you young cubs!"

"Sorry," said Bert. "We didn't mean to run into you."

The surly fellow took a threatening step towards the boys, but suddenly turned and sneaked off as a policeman came around the corner.

"I bet that man was after the dog, too," said Bert. "And he acted afraid of the policeman. I don't like him."

"Golly, where did the dog go?" cried Freddie.

"There it is, running down that alleyway," called Bert. "Come on, Freddie."

The animal stopped to rest, but when it saw the boys it started on again. A merry chase it led them, up one street and down another, doubling back upon its own trail, darting into alleyways so that the boys were afraid all the time of losing it entirely.

At last they ran it to earth in a narrow space between two stores. Here there was no way for the dog to escape except by the path it had come in, and this was blocked by the sturdy figures of Bert and Freddie Bobbsey.

The animal looked at them, its ears pointed forward. Then it seemed to make up its mind. It dropped the package from its teeth and looked at the boys as if to say, "Well, here it is. Now, what do you want to do with it?"

"Good dog!" Bert approached very quietly, and held out his hand. "Nice doggie. Lie down and be good."

The animal did as he was told, but looked at Bert very closely, his ears still pointed forward.

"My! I hope he doesn't pick up the package and run again," said Freddie.

Bert put out his hand carefully and grasped the little bundle. The dog did not try to stop him, but began to wag its tail gently as if to tell Bert that the boy was quite welcome to the prize if he wanted it.

Bert straightened up, a little leather bag in his hand.

"What is it?" asked Freddie.

"Looks as if it fell out of somebody's purse," said Bert. "It has a zipper top."

"Let's open it," cried Freddie. "Maybe there's a hunting-knife inside."

"It's too small," replied his brother.

When the pouch was opened the brothers found something quite different from a hunting-knife. There was no money, though there was a loose rubber band that looked as though it might, at some time, have been placed around a roll of bills. What interested Bert and Freddie most of all was a small bag with a draw-string top.

After some fumbling Bert managed to open the little purse, and out of it there tumbled a dozen pieces of fine jewellery—several rings set with sparkling stones, two handsome bar-pins, a pair of ear-rings, and an old-fashioned locket with a monogram on it.

"Those are 'nitials, aren't they?" asked Freddie, trying to trace the letters with his finger. "What do they say, Bert?"

"H. L.," read his brother. He was thoughtful for a moment. "Maybe that 'L' stands for Lamson," he said slowly. "It might, Freddie, you know."

"Then the locket would belong to Miss Lamson, wouldn't it?" cried the little boy. "Golly!"

"Yes, the locket would belong to her and so would all this jewellery," replied Bert.

"My, won't she be glad to get it back!" said Freddie. "Let's go tell her, Bert."

However, when the boys got back to the place where they had left the little group they found no trace of Miss Lamson, their father, Nan, or Flossie.

"They must have gone home," said Freddie sadly. "Now what shall we do, Bert?"

"Go home too, I guess," said his brother. "We can show the bag to Mother and Daddy and they will know just what to do with it."

Mr. and Mrs. Bobbsey, Nan and Flossie were all very much interested in what Freddie and Bert had picked up. Mrs. Bobbsey said at once that they must try to find Miss Lamson and see if the jewellery belonged to her.

"But we don't know where she lives," said Nan.

"Then we'll have to advertise in the newspaper," said her father.

"Oh, let's!" cried Freddie. "We can go around to the newspaper office right now."

Mrs. Bobbsey shook her head. "You will have to wait until morning," she said. "Dinner will be ready very soon. And Freddie, do run upstairs and wash your hands. They're frightfully dirty."

A few moments later, just before Dinah came in to announce dinner, Freddie went over to his mother and thrust one of his nice, clean hands into her own.

"I'm sorry, Mother, about your fur coat," he said manfully. " I didn't mean to tear it. I just put it on to find out what it felt like to be a trapper."

"And now do you know how it feels to be a trapper?" asked Mrs. Bobbsey, smiling at him.

"We-el, I don't know," said the little boy. "I don't suppose trappers fall downstairs very often."

Nan and Bert laughed at this, and Mrs. Bobbsey gave Freddie's sturdy little shoulders a hug.

"I'll forgive you this time," she told him, "but don't do it again. Fur coats are expensive, you know."

The next day was Saturday, and the children started off bright and early to take their advertisement to the newspaper office. On the way they had to pass Mr. Palant's fur shop. As they paused for a moment to look at the window display, the man saw them, and came to the door.

"I had several customers after you left yesterday," he told them, rubbing his hands with pleasure. "Two of them bought scarfs and one ordered a fur coat, all because of your window display. I thing I shall have to take you youngsters into business with me if this keeps up!" he teased.

Naturally, the Bobbsey twins were delighted to hear that the furrier's business was better. They said good-bye to Mr. Palant, and continued to the newspaper office. As they went on they discussed their father's Northern trip, and wished again that they might be allowed to go with him.

"Oh, I do so hope we can," sighed Flossie. "I want to see a real Eskimo igloo more than anything else in the world."

"I want to see how the Eskimos live," said Freddie. "They look nice and jolly. They must have lots of fun."

As they were about to enter the newspaper office, the little boy pulled his brother by the sleeve.

"Look, Bert," he cried, "there's that man we ran into yesterday. My, he looks like a bad person. Maybe he's going to hurt us!"

CHAPTER IV

THE BROKEN KITE

BERT turned around and saw the mean-looking fellow coming towards them.

"He's—he's following us," whispered Freddie, grabbing his brother's hand.

"I wonder what he wants," said Bert nervously. "Come, we'll hurry inside."

The man must have decided not to go into the newspaper building, for he turned about and disappeared in the crowd on the pavement.

"Oh, I'm glad," said Freddie. "Where are the girls?"

Nan and Flossie had gone on ahead and had reached a long counter by the time the boys caught up with them. The children had to wait, for several people were there. One old lady was saying:

"Yes, some bad dog chased my cat away and she hasn't come back yet. And I miss her. I must have her back. I can't get along without her."

The man behind the counter smiled. "You don't want to put all that in your ad, do you? It would cost a lot."

Flossie giggled so loudly that Nan had to stop her sister.

"Won't you wait on me, please?" asked a fat man, shoving himself ahead of several people. "I'm in a great hurry. I lost my wife's umbrella and if I don't get it back she'll be mad about it."

"I think probably all these folks are in a hurry," said the clerk. "Please wait for your turn."

Flossie giggled again, and Freddie, who was trying to act grown-up, took hold of his twin's arm. "Don't be silly. Why do girls always have to laugh at everything?"

Presently the newspaper man spoke to Nan, saying, "And now, what can I do for you, Miss?"

The Bobbsey girl opened her purse and took out a slip on which her mother had written an advertisement.

"We want this put into your paper," she said. "How much will it cost?"

Soon Nan had paid for the item. The clerk rolled up the slip, opened a little cover to a long brass tube, and put the paper inside.

"What's going to happen now?" asked Bert of the worker.

"Your ad is being carried to a big room downstairs where the typing and printing are done. By this time a man has your note and is setting it up."

Suddenly Freddie Bobbsey cried out, "Wait! Wait! Don't put the ad in!"

"What's that?" asked the fellow.

"Why, Freddie," said Nan, "what are you talking about?"

"Miss Lamson," answered the little boy. "There she is—over there!"

"Miss Lamson!" cried the others.

Flossie ran forward and caught the teacher's hand in her chubby fist.

"We wanted to see you," said the little girl. "We just put a piece in the paper for you."

"Well, that's strange," said Miss Lamson, smiling. "I have just put an ad in there myself—for my lost money bag."

"But we've found it!" cried Flossie. "At least, Bert and Freddie did."

"You found my bag?" she cried delightedly. "Was the money in it, and the jewels, too?"

"Well, we picked up one, with the initials 'H.L.' on a locket. There were some rings and things in it," the older Bobbsey boy said, "but there wasn't any money."

Miss Lamson's face fell. After a moment she said, "Well, I suppose I must consider myself lucky to get back my jewels. I suppose whoever found the bag in the first place put my roll of bills in his—or her—pocket."

"Why don't you come home with us, Miss Lamson?" Nan suggested. "I know Mother will be glad to see you, and then Bert and Freddie can give you back your property."

"And I have yet to hear how it was found," said Miss Lamson. "How about the ad you were going to put in the paper?" she asked, as they turned away. "I thought you said——"

The man at the desk was very nice and gave back the money to Nan. He said he would send a note downstairs and have the ad taken out right away.

"We didn't know where you lived," said Flossie to Miss Lamson.

"I left my address at the restaurant where I had tea, don't you remember? All you needed to do was to go there and ask the girl at the desk."

The children looked crestfallen.

"We never thought of that," said Nan.

"Well, never mind," smiled Miss Lamson. "The main thing is that the lost is found. While we walk up to your house I'd like to hear all about it," she said to Bert and Freddie.

The boys were only too glad to tell the story. Miss Lamson asked them many questions, and seemed to be particularly interested in the rough-looking man into whom Bert and Freddie had bumped and who had shown fight until the sight of a policeman had sent him off in a hurry.

"Do you suppose that man was following the dog, too?" she said thoughtfully. "Could he possibly have known what it was the animal was carrying in his mouth?"

"I think he did," replied Bert.

Arriving at the Bobbsey home, Miss Lamson was ushered into the pleasant living-room, and greeted cordially by Mrs. Bobbsey.

"I feel that I know you very well already, Miss Lamson," said the twins' mother. "My children have talked of almost no one else since yesterday. We should like to have you stay to luncheon and tell us about your interesting work at the Hudson Bay settlement."

Miss Lamson consented. Freddie brought in the

bag which he and Bert had rescued from the police dog the previous day. With an exclamation of pleasure she turned its contents into her lap.

"My rings are all here and the pins, too," she said, counting them carefully. "Yes, all my jewellery is here, for which I should be thankful. Now, if my money had been there as well—however, I suppose that is too much to expect," she finished with a cheerful smile. "I guess I must make up my mind to accept that loss. And now, let's talk about a more pleasant subject. How would you like to have me tell you about Cold Star settlement?"

"Oh, oh, please do!" cried Flossie.

"I'll get the chairs!" offered Freddie.

The children gathered in a semicircle about their new friend, and from then until it was time to eat Miss Lamson kept them entertained with tales of the North and the people who make their homes in that land, where they have snow and ice most of the year. When Dinah came to announce that luncheon was ready she had to speak twice before anyone heard her!

After the meal was over, Charlie Mason and Ted Blake came to call for Bert and Freddie. They were neighbourhood children who had long been friends of the Bobbsey boys. They wanted Bert and Freddie to go with them to an open field near the school.

"We are going to fly our new kites," said Charlie Mason. "Come on, fellows. Hurry up!"

Freddie and Bert were torn between a desire to fly their new kites and an urgent wish to hear more about Hudson Bay. The kites finally won, and the Bobbsey boys said good-bye to their mother and Miss Lamson,

promising to get back again before the teacher should
leave for home.

At the playing-field, which was swarming with
other youngsters who were out to celebrate the holiday
from school, the boys soon got their kites in the air.
Bert's was very balky. It kept falling down just when
he thought he had it well started on its flight. Each
time he would have to run with it across the field in the
hope that a gust of wind might catch it and toss it
skywards.

On one such occasion, while he was running and
not paying very much attention to anything ahead of
him, he looked up just in time to avoid bumping full
tilt into a man who was crossing the field and coming
towards him.

As Bert swerved to one side, the big kite came sail-
ing down, covering both himself and the man with a
mass of paper, wood framework, and string. Freddie
drew in his kite and hurried up the field towards his
brother, who floundered about and tugged at the
string that bound his feet and ankles.

"I'm sorry——" Bert began, then stopped and
stared.

The man he had just run down, and who stood
entangled by string and the long white tail of the kite,
was the same mean-looking person he had bumped
into the day before during his mad dash after the
police dog!

Bert wanted to laugh because the follow really did
look very funny with the tail of the kite wrapped
around his throat like a bandage. Perhaps he did smile
just a little; at any rate, something threw the man into

a terrible rage. He glowered at Bert, and began tearing with both hands at the kite cloth about his throat.

"Don't tear it, please," begged the boy. "Here, I'll help you get it off."

He started to do so, but the violent fellow gave the lad a shove that almost knocked him off his feet.

"None of your tricks now," growled the rascal. "I'll get it off myself, and no thanks to you. And I'll break your old kite for you, too. Take that—and that!"

Before Bert's outraged eyes the man grasped the precious kite in his strong, thick hands, and tore it apart. Not content with that, he snatched the kites of the other three boys, who had come up by this time. Before they realized what he was about, he had ruined them also, stamping the wreckage into the ground with his muddy shoe.

"Here, you let that alone!" cried Freddie, almost in tears. "It's a brand new kite! You stop that, you— you——"

"Here, what's all this!"

The voice was one of authority. The boys turned to see the policeman who stood on duty every week-day at the south corner of the school. He was a nice man, broad shouldered and ruddy faced, and was well liked by all the children. Now the boys hailed him as a friend.

"That man broke our kites," cried Freddie. "He did it on purpose."

"They were new ones, too," said Ted Blake. "We bought them at the store only yesterday."

At the appearance of the officer, a curious change came over the stranger. His anger fell from him and he suddenly looked frightened. He started to edge away from the group, but the heavy hand of the policeman dropped on the man's shoulder and stopped him.

"Up to your old tricks, Beb Deet! Bullying a parcel of young lads that can't fight back. Ruinin' property that doesn't belong to you, too. It's a wonder you're not ashamed of yourself."

"The kid run me down, Officer," said Beb Deet in a whining voice. "I got mad and broke his kite."

"He broke mine, too," said Freddie.

"And mine!"

"And mine!" from Charlie and Ted.

"Well, now, if you was to pay for these kites, the lads might let you off," said the policeman, his hand very heavy on Beb Deet's shoulder. "I'd hate to arrest you, you know, for such a little thing."

Grumbling, the man took out a shabby wallet and from it drew a one dollar bill. This he handed to Bert, scowling as he did so.

"All right, now you be off," said the officer, giving Deet's shoulder a shake. "And I hope this is the last I'll be seein' of you for many a day."

After the boys had thanked the good-hearted policeman and he had gone on his way, Bert left his friends and ran home. He had not told them that his curiosity had been aroused by seeing a big roll of bills in Beb Deet's wallet. But that is just what had happened.

Now Bert was eager to tell Nan of his suspicions, and ask her advice. Nan was always so level-headed and sensible. She would know just what to do. When he got to the Bobbsey house, he called his sister and told her all about this new encounter with Beb Deet.

"It seems strange that such a poor man should have a thick roll of bills in his pocket. I think he may have stolen the money. If that is the case, then it may be Miss Lamson's."

"If your hunch is right, this Beb Deet must have been in the restaurant at the same time Miss Lamson was," said Nan thoughtfully. "You wait here, Bert, while I get my coat."

"What for?" asked her brother.

"We are going to that restaurant," Nan replied.

When they got there, the clerk at the desk greeted them. In reply to their questions she admitted that a man answering Beb Deet's description had visited the place the previous day. By checking up on time, and by questioning the waitress who had served Miss Lamson, the children became certain that the mean man—or a person remarkably like him—had been in the eating place at the same time as had the teacher, and that he had sat at a table close to the one occupied by her.

"When Miss Lamson stood up she forgot her purse," said Nan, trying to figure out what might have happened.

"And Beb Deet picked up the purse, took out the inside bag with the money and jewellery in it, and threw the purse away!"

"Where Freddie found it behind the umbrella stand," finished Nan triumphantly. "Let's run home, Bert, and tell Miss Lamson we think we know who has her money!"

CHAPTER V

CAUGHT!

WHEN Bert and Nan reached home with their great news, they were relieved to find that Miss Lamson had not left. The teacher and Mrs. Bobbsey greeted the children with smiles, and their mother asked them if anything unusual had happened.

"You look as if you were up to something," she said, as she noticed their dancing eyes.

"We are," said Nan gaily. "A nice thing, though, and I think Miss Lamson will like what we are going to tell her."

The teacher was more than interested in their story.

"This Beb Deet sounds like a dangerous person," she said. "He could very well have picked up my purse after I left the restaurant, and helped himself to its contents. I wonder, though, why he didn't keep the bag with all the jewellery in it. It is really valuable."

"Maybe he dropped that by mistake on the way to the street," Nan suggested.

"And the police dog picked it up and ran off with it," added Bert. "Don't you see," he went on, struck by a sudden thought, "that would explain why Beb Deet was chasing the dog at the same time we were. He wanted to get back the bag!"

"It sounds plausible," Miss Lamson agreed. "It certainly looks as if this man has my money. If he doesn't return it in a day or two, I shall have to notify the police."

At this moment Daddy Bobbsey's step was heard at the front door, and the children rushed out to tell him about their day's adventures and the mystery they thought they might have solved.

"Well, Richard, you're home early," said Mrs. Bobbsey as her tall husband bent to kiss her.

Mr. Bobbsey greeted Miss Lamson, and said, "I'm glad you are here, for I think you can give me some good advice about the North country."

"I'll be delighted to help you," the teacher replied. "Are you going to make the trip?"

"Yes," said Mr. Bobbsey. "I feel I must look for Mr. Weller. If he isn't found by a certain time he will not receive a lot of money that should come to him from someone who died."

"Are you sure he's around Hudson Bay?" asked Bert.

"Maybe he lives in an igloo," whispered Flossie to her mother.

Mr. Bobbsey went on, "Yes, Bert, he's in that part of Canada. And if I'm to find him I'll have to start soon, for winter sets in early up there and the boats stop running."

"It would be dreadful, Daddy," said Nan, "if you got up there and couldn't come back until next summer!"

"Why don't you wait until spring?" suggested Mrs. Bobbsey.

"It would be too late," her husband replied. "If I wait that long, I couldn't find Mr. Weller in time. That would look bad for me, for I have been given the job of seeing that he gets his money. If I don't hunt for him, people will think I am mean and don't want the man to have it."

"You're never mean," said Flossie loyally. "Nobody could say that!"

"Well, little fat fairy," laughed her daddy, picking up the small girl, "you're my pal. And what would you say if I should tell you that I almost decided to take you and the others with me on this trip, but I'm afraid now that I can't do it."

"Oh! Do take us!"

"Please!"

"Why not?"

"One at a time," begged Mr. Bobbsey. "Now, Miss Lamson, will you tell me what you think of my idea? Isn't it too late in the year to start out with my family?"

"Not if you go right away," the young woman replied.

"But where could Mrs. Bobbsey and the children stay while I travel about?" objected the twins' father. "The region around the northern part of Hudson Bay doesn't have hotels and boarding houses."

"Oh, you will stay at the Cold Star settlement!" announced Miss Lamson.

"We couldn't do that," said Mrs. Bobbsey quickly. "Six extra people! I'm sure there wouldn't be room enough. Thank you, but we really couldn't impose upon you."

"I'm sure you wouldn't mind being a little crowded," said Miss Lamson. "It would be a wonderful experience for the children, and they have done so much for me, I should like the chance to do something for them."

Mr. Bobbsey looked at his wife and then at each of his children. The twins looked as if they would have to burst out any minute. They were trying their utmost not to interrupt. Finally their mother spoke up.

"All right. I'll consent, Miss Lamson, we are very grateful."

"Whee!" yelled Freddie.

"Oh, Mother, that's swell!" burst out Bert.

As Flossie gave her father an extra hard squeeze, Nan went over to the teacher.

"Maybe I can help you in your work," she said. "I guess I have been to school more than the Eskimo children have."

"That's very sweet of you, my dear," replied the settlement worker. "I believe you can."

Presently the children left the room to talk over the coming trip. The fascinating North country, with all its scenes, its thrills and delights, was coming very close to them. Within a short time now, a week or two at the most, they would actually be there, and see with their own eyes the vast stretches of ice and snow, the grey sky, the scattered villages, all the strange, almost dream-like sights of a new land.

"I hope Daddy lets us live in an igloo," said Flossie, "with oil lamps and fat to eat, and maybe a nice Eskimo dog or two to keep us company."

"The dog part sounds all right," said Bert. "But I don't know how I'd like the lamps and the fat to eat."

Flossie giggled.

"You wouldn't have to eat the lamps," she pointed out.

Bert gave her a disgusted, big-brother look.

"Silly!" he said. "You know what I meant."

At the beginning of the next week, Miss Lamson had heard nothing about her lost money, so on Monday afternoon the children set out after school hours to try to find Beb Deet.

The policeman on duty at the corner said upon questioning that he had seen the mean man only a short time before hanging about the building, and had sent him away. The officer pointed out the direction Deet had taken, but told the children to keep away from the ugly fellow.

"He's a bad one, and no mistake. You'd best be leavin' him alone."

The Bobbseys thanked the policeman, but went on their way after the man, feeling that they must find him. They asked about him as they walked along, and finally trailed him to the outskirts of the town. There they came to a wood where they felt sure they had lost sight of him. However, they continued their search, and were finally rewarded with a glimpse of the man.

"Be careful," warned Bert, catching Freddie and Flossie by their hands. "Don't make a sound! Beb Deet is right over there under that tree. If we can slip up on him without letting him know we're here, we may learn something interesting."

The younger children promised to be very quiet, and carefully crept up on Deet until they were within a few feet of him. They were still hidden by the trees, and Freddie and Flossie fairly held their breaths to keep from making a sound.

Nan peered around a tree trunk, and her eyes nearly popped from her head. Beb Deet was holding in his hand a fat roll of bills. Now, as Nan and the other children watched, he began to count the money.

Suddenly something white near Bert's feet caught the boy's attention. It was a handkerchief, a lady's handkerchief. The lad stooped quickly and picked it up. In the corner was a monogram with two letters.

"H. L.," read Bert.

The boy realized now that the bit of linen must belong to Miss Lamson. No doubt this same handkerchief had come from the pocket of Beb Deet just now. Then, reasoned Bert, the roll of bills must belong to the young lady, too. He handed the handkerchief to Nan, his finger on the monogram. She nodded excitedly and pointed to Deet.

The man had restored the money and other articles to his pocket. Now he settled himself with his back against a tree, his shabby hat pulled down over his eyes, as though he was preparing to take a good rest.

Quietly the children moved away from the spot. They quickened their pace when they were sure the fellow could not hear them. By the time they reached the end of the woods they were almost running in their eagerness to find someone in authority to whom they might tell their story.

As luck would have it, the first person they saw when they reached town was a policeman, calmly pacing up and down his beat. He listened to their story, and willingly returned with them to the place where they had left Beb Deet.

The man was there, sound asleep. The patrolman placed a hand on his shoulder and shook him into wakefulness.

"Better come along with me," he said. "I think you're wanted at headquarters."

Deet shook off the officer's hand and jumped to his feet.

"What do you want me for?" he growled. "I ain't done nothing."

"We'll see about that," said the officer. He twirled his night-stick and tightened his grip on the fellow's arm. "*Now* will you come along quietly, or will I have to use force? Perhaps these will help make up your mind for you!"

In a flash the policeman took a pair of handcuffs from his pocket and hooked them about Beb Deet's wrists. The man made no further protest. On the way to the station the officer telephoned to Miss Lamson's address, which he had learned from the twins, and asked that lady to meet them at headquarters.

"Now, Miss," he said to the teacher a little later, "this man is accused of stealing something belonging to you. We have taken a large roll of bills from him and several other articles. If you can identify them, we will be glad to turn them over to you."

Miss Lamson did so, naming to within a few dollars

the amount found in Deet's pocket. She mentioned also the handkerchief marked with her monogram, a pair of eyeglasses, and a railway ticket to Canada, which she had bought on the morning of the very day her purse was taken.

"I guess you win, Miss," said the officer. "Looks as if all these things are yours. Mighty glad you'll be to get them back, I shouldn't wonder."

"Indeed I am, Officer. Thank you very much."

"It isn't I you should be thanking," said the officer with a smiling glance at the Bobbseys. "It's these youngsters who gave me the tip and really made the arrest. Great kids they are, and no mistake."

"You don't have to tell me that," said Miss Lamson with a warm smile. "And now I want them to come to my home with me."

The twins stayed just long enough to see Beb Deet hustled through the door that led to the jail; then they turned away with the teacher.

"Now we can all be real happy going to Eskimo Land together," said Freddie, " 'cause you have your money back."

"And seeing the igloos," added Flossie.

When the twins reached the home of the teacher's parents, they were asked to sit down and wait while Miss Lamson went upstairs to get something.

"I have a little present for you," she said. "It is something I prize very much, for my Eskimo people made it for me, and they don't have tools to work with the way you do."

She left the room and was gone for several minutes.

"What do you suppose it is?" asked Flossie.

"I wonder," said Nan.

When Miss Lamson returned she was carrying a bag in one hand. The children crowded round her.

"Now what do you think of this?" she asked.

As she spoke, the settlement worker drew from the parcel a small toy sleigh drawn by four huskies. As you probably know, these are the dogs that native traders use to draw sleds over great wastes of ice and snow in the countries of the far North. They are big beasts, shaggy and powerful, usually deeply devoted to their masters, and extremely intelligent about finding their way over frozen trails.

Flossie clapped her hands with delight when she saw the pretty toy.

"Oh, please, may I play with it?" begged the little girl. "I'll be very, very careful of it."

"Huskies must surely be swell dogs," said Freddie. "I'd like to have one for a pet."

"Husky puppies are clever," Miss Lamson agreed. "When they are little they look like tiny shaggy teddy-bears."

"Do you think we'll see some when we get to Eskimo Land?" asked Flossie.

"Certainly you will."

The children thanked the teacher and hurried home to show their gift.

"It is very attractive," said Mrs. Bobbsey, who was busy sewing for the coming trip. "Take good care of it."

Several days of shopping followed. At last all the baggage was packed, including Mrs. Bobbsey's fur coat, which had been fixed by Mr. Palant and was once more as good as new. Last-minute good-byes were said to schoolmates by the children.

Now Mr. and Mrs. Bobbsey, the Bobbsey twins, and Miss Helen Lamson stood on the Lakeport station platform. They were waiting for the train to take them towards Eskimo Land!

CHAPTER VI

FREDDIE'S JOKE

A GREAT many of the Bobbseys' friends had gathered to see them off. Grace Lavine and Nellie Parks were there to say good-bye to Nan, and to wish her a happy journey.

Charlie Mason and John Marsh had turned up, the former with a brand-new kite he had brought for Bert's inspection.

"I bet there isn't much kite-flying in Eskimo Land," grinned Charlie.

"Guess not," Bert replied. "We can go walrus-hunting instead."

"Some people have all the luck in the world," said John a little enviously. "Who cares for a kite when he can shoot walruses?"

At the last minute little Susie Larker arrived with her parents. She wanted to say good-bye to Flossie, she said, and to beg her not to turn into an Eskimo so she would have to stay up North and live in an igloo.

It was all very gay and exciting. In spite of the fact that they were going away on such a marvellous adventure, the Bobbsey twins could not help but feel a little sorry that they were forced to part with all their friends, even though it would not be for very long.

"Wouldn't it be nice if we could take them all with us?" asked Flossie.

The train then came rumbling into the station, and Daddy Bobbsey managed to herd his flock aboard without leaving any of them behind.

Freddie and Flossie leaned out of the window and waved to the group on the platform. But they had to be pulled inside as the train began to move. At last they found their places. As the train gathered speed, rumbling rhythmically over the rails, it was borne in upon the twins that their journey really had begun. They were actually on their way to Eskimo Land!

It was fun getting settled, Nan and Bert in one seat, Flossie and Freddie facing them across the way. Mother and Daddy Bobbsey and Miss Lamson occupied the next pair of seats. In the one beside Miss Lamson was a basket of fruit Daddy had bought for them all, and Mother's lap was overflowing with magazines and a big box of chocolates.

"Oh!" said Flossie. "This will be fun!"

A little later Miss Lamson called them over to her.

"I thought you might like to see some toys I have bought for my little Eskimo friends," said the teacher.

"Oh, we surely would!" cried Flossie.

"Where are they?" Freddie wanted to know.

"Right here in this suit-case," said Miss Lamson. "Now, did you ever see anything sweeter than this?"

In a box was a row of dolls of twelve different countries of the world in their native dress. Alongside

each one was a house or a hut like those in which the
people of those lands live.

"Oh, see that darling Chinese one," cried Nan.

"What do you call its house with all those roofs?"
asked Freddie.

"A pagoda," replied Miss Lamson.

"Look at that coloured doll with the grass skirt,"
said Bert. "And the grass hut. I'll bet the Eskimos
will wonder why those Africans don't freeze to
death!"

"You might tell them," suggested the teacher with
a laugh. "You know, Nan offered to help me with
my work."

"I have an idea!" said Bert. "I brought along my
bank, which is made like a very tall office-building.
Sixty-four stories high! I'm going to give it to you
to put with these things."

"Will you leave the money in it?" teased Nan.

"Well, no, I guess not," said Bert.

"Eskimos haven't much need of money, anyway,"
said Miss Lamson. "They get along without it by
hunting their own food, making their own clothes,
and building their own houses out of whatever is at
hand."

"That is a good thing to do," said Flossie.

"Here's another toy I bought for my little Eskimo
friends." Miss Lamson groped among her packages
and brought forth, of all things, a small, very bright
red fire-engine!

Mrs. Bobbsey laughed as young Freddie reached
eagerly for the shining toy.

"One might know Freddie would like that," she

commented. "He loves anything that squirts water."

"Freddie wants to be a fireman when he grows up," laughed Nan.

"You can't get water in this engine," said the little boy. "A toy like that can't be much good."

"Freddie!" reproved his mother.

"Oh, I'm sorry," said the little boy with a glance at Miss Lamson. "It probably is a very nice fire-engine. I'm sure the Eskimo children will like it."

"You see, the little Eskimos don't know anything about fire-engines," Miss Lamson explained, "so this toy will be a great novelty to them. Now, I have something here that will probably interest you even even more."

Once again Miss Lamson reached down into the wonderful bag, and this time she brought forth the sort of toy which is in answer to almost every child's dream. It was a music-box, perfect in each detail, even to the crank on the outside which, when wound up, made the tiny machine inside play little tunes. The case was shiny black with delicate pink flowers painted on the top.

"How pretty!" cried Nan, delighted. "Does it really play pieces?"

"I should say so," returned Miss Lamson. "Listen!"

The teacher pushed a switch at the side of the box, and from it there came, like the tinkling of fairy bells, the soft, sweet strains of "The Last Rose of Summer". The children listened, enchanted, until the final bell-like note had died away.

"Does it play any other pieces?" asked Flossie.

Miss Lamson nodded, and placed a finger to her lips.

"Listen!" she said.

This time the tune was "Annie Laurie". The well-loved melody was followed by "The Old Grey Mare."

"And that's all," said Miss Lamson when the notes came to an end. "Do you think my little Eskimo friends will like it?"

"They will love it," said Nan. "May I have it for a little while, Miss Lamson? I'll be very, very careful of it."

The nice lady assented, and again reached into the wonderful bag.

"I have something here that should be of interest to a big boy," she said, glancing at Bert. "It may not be able to shoot things, but it certainly looks as if it could."

"A gun!" said Bert, leaning forward eagerly.

And that's just what it was; a perfect model of a repeating rifle, yet so small it seemed unbelievable that every little detail could be so perfect.

"This is swell," said the boy, turning the tiny weapon over and over lovingly in his hands. "I wish Dad would let me have a real gun."

"He will when he is quite sure you won't shoot yourself with it," said Mrs. Bobbsey.

"I wouldn't anyway," said Bert, gazing at the toy rifle. "This is great. Do you mind if I look at it a little while, Miss Lamson?"

She did not mind in the least. The other children might keep the toys for a time, she said, if they would be very careful and not break them. After a word of caution from Mrs. Bobbsey, the twins returned to their own seats to enjoy the treasures.

A little later Mr. Bobbsey took his family and Miss Lamson to luncheon in the dining-car. It was a very good meal, and the twins were sorry when it came to an end.

Between delight in the toys Miss Lamson had lent them and the pleasure of watching the changing scenery from the train windows, the hours of that first day flew away far too swiftly to suit the Bobbsey twins.

Once Nan gently nudged her mother. "Freddie's asleep," she said.

Sure enough, the small boy had laid his curly head on the window-sill, while the rest of him was cuddled up in the corner of the seat.

"I think I'll go move him," said Mrs. Bobbsey. "Bert, you had better be seated somewhere else."

Very gently she stretched out her little son across the seat and put a coat under his head for a pillow. In this position Freddie slept for nearly two hours. The result was that when bed-time came he was wide awake. However, when the other children were tucked in, Mrs. Bobbsey insisted that he go to bed in an upper berth with Bert.

"I'm not going to sleep, though," announced Freddie.

His father and mother settled down to read for a while. Suddenly there was a sound which startled them.

Tinkle! Tinkle! Tra-la-la!

"What's that?" asked Mr. Bobbsey.

"I can't imagine," said his wife, "but it seems as if it came from the boys' berth."

All was quiet for a while, then the sounds came again. This time it was faint music.

"Richard, you better look in and see what those boys are up to," said Mrs. Bobbsey.

The twins' father did so, and found everything peaceful. The eyes of Bert and Freddie were tightly closed. The lads were evidently sound asleep.

The older Bobbseys had just started again to read, when a tune began to be played.

"Hey, stop that music, will you?" called a gruff voice from a near-by berth. "I want to sleep."

Mrs. Bobbsey whispered to her husband, "It's my guess that Freddie is playing a joke. Tiptoe over and stand near his berth."

Mr. Bobbsey did this. Sure enough! In a few moments some sweet music began to come from the bed where Bert and Freddie were supposed to be sleeping.

"Stop that!" cried someone up the car. "We don't want to be disturbed!"

Quickly Mr. Bobbsey pulled aside the curtain, just in time to see his small son putting something under his pillow.

"Freddie! What are you doing?"

The little fellow tried to pretend to be asleep, but he could not fool his father again. Mr. Bobbsey reached under the pillow and drew out a little object.

Miss Lamson's music-box.

"I—I didn't mean to bother anybody," said Freddie. "I couldn't go to sleep and I wanted to have some fun."

His father said nothing except, "Good night, Freddie. You go right to sleep!"

The next few days of the trip passed by as swiftly and pleasantly as had the first ones. Then, one day, when the train had stopped for water and the children were out on the platform getting a little exercise, the roar of an aeroplane-motor caused them all to look overhead.

"I believe that plane's in trouble," said Bert after a moment. "Something's wrong with it, that's sure."

"Oo—oo," screamed Flossie. "It's going to fall!"

CHAPTER VII

THE PLANE CRASH

AS Bert spoke, the motors of the aeroplane suddenly went dead. The machine seemed to stand still for a moment, like a bird that has been shot while flying, then began to fall towards the ground.

"I can't look!" Flossie cried out, and clapped both her chubby hands to her eyes.

Nan grew white and turned away. Freddie stared at the tumbling plane as though he could not drag his eyes away from it.

"The pilot has jumped!" cried Bert. "He has his parachute!"

By this time a crowd had gathered on the platform. Nan felt a hand on her shoulder and looked up to see Miss Helen Lamson.

"It's all right," said the teacher kindly. "The pilot is safe. His parachute opened, you see."

As she spoke, there came a sharp crash. Cries and groans broke from the lips of the watchers.

"There goes the plane!" cried everyone as it went into a tree.

"Smashed to bits," said another. "Hope no one is in it."

Slowly the parachute came down. The **man**

dangled like an insect beneath a great white umbrella. As he neared the earth, his figure seemed to grow larger. Finally, even his face could be seen as he bent his head to stare down at the ground.

"That must be fun," said Flossie with a clap of her hands. "Like being up in a big swing."

"Golly, I believe he's going to land right near us," said Freddie. He began to run towards the edge of the platform, but Nan held him back.

"Better stay here," she said. "You might get caught under the parachute."

The little boy wiggled out of his sister's grasp, jumped off the platform, and made straight for the pilot.

"Come back! Come back!"

Freddie was now directly beneath the big white cloud that was coming down.

"Look out!" called the pilot. "Run away!"

But the young Bobbsey lad did not move. He was too thrilled. As the airman touched his feet to the ground, he was pulled along for a few yards by the parachute. Then the great folds settled down over him, and over Freddie as well.

"Ugh!" Spl-uff!" sputtered the little boy. "I'm choking!"

As some of the crowd on the platform hurried towards the crashed plane, others, including Miss Lamson, Bert, Nan, and Flossie, ran to the pilot and Freddie.

"I know that man!" cried the teacher. "It's Alfred Faber, unless I am very much mistaken."

Quickly willing hands pulled the smothering folds of the parachute away from the two.

"Are you all right?" Nan asked Freddie, hugging her little brother.

"Oh, sure," he replied.

Other hands, no less willing, helped the pilot to his feet. Friendly voices asked him if he were hurt.

"I'm—all—right," he answered.

"Was anyone else in the plane?"

"No, there wasn't, I'm glad to say."

The young man shook himself, wiped some dust from his face with the back of his sleeve, and smiled at them.

"I'm pretty dirty," he said. "Tried to fix the machine but I couldn't. Sorry she had to crash."

He fumbled with the straps that bound the life-saving device to his shoulders. Bert Bobbsey sprang forward to help him.

"Let me, sir," he begged. "I know how these straps work."

"Thanks, son." The flier staggered a little and flung an arm over Bert's sturdy shoulders. "Guess I can do with a little help after all."

At this point Miss Lamson stepped forward. She took the flier by the arm and smiled at him.

"Why, Helen. How did you get here?" The young man's face lighted up and Nan thought he looked very pleased indeed to see Miss Lamson.

"That's a long story," said the teacher. "Come over to the train and I will tell you about it. At the same time, we will try to find out if you really are all right. Sure you have no broken bones?"

"I'll come along with you," grinned the flier,

"because I want to hear how you happen to be in this place. But I haven't any broken bones."

Everyone in the train had come out and wanted to hear about the accident. Mr. and Mrs. Bobbsey were particularly interested in knowing what the pilot was going to do.

"I think I'd better be getting to the nearest settlement," said the flier. "I'll have to find someone to help me get my plane out of the tree."

"Golly, can you?" asked Freddie.

"But it was all smashed to bits," said Flossie.

The flier shook his head.

"No. One wing is damaged and the motors will stand overhauling. But I think the machine can be made to fly."

"Aren't you afraid to go up after what happened?" asked Nan.

"Fliers can't afford to be afraid," said the young man with a laugh. "The sooner one gets in the air after a smash like this, the better."

The pilot and Miss Lamson walked off to have a few words alone. In a few moments there came a shrill whistle from the engine.

"We're going to go!" shouted Freddie.

"Well, so long, everybody," called Al Faber, the pilot. "I'll be seeing you at Cold Star."

The twins were sorry to see the aviator leave. They noticed that Miss Lamson seemed sorry, too, and that she followed the young man to the train door as though very anxious for his welfare.

Then they heard the guard outside warning all the passengers, and they knew that the train was about to start.

"All aboard!" he shouted.

When Miss Lamson returned, the twins beset her with questions about the airman. Did she know him well? Was he on his way to Hudson Bay now? Would they really see him again after they reached Cold Star?

To all their questions Miss Lamson answered "yes". She seemed rather thoughtful and absent-minded, however, and the twins guessed that she was worrying about Al Faber. Perhaps she was wondering whether he would be able to get his plane down out of the tree and whether, even if he did, he would manage to reach Cold Star in safety. The twins hoped he would, for they had begun to like him very much.

Now the trip began to enter its last stages. The scenery from the windows became more and more wintry as the train went farther and farther north. Whenever it stopped, and the passengers got out to "exercise themselves", they had to bundle up well in heavy coats against the cold blasts.

Mrs. Bobbsey found her fur coat very comfortable. Freddie and Flossie wound their mufflers tightly about their necks and wished they were far enough north to buy the furs Mr. Bobbsey had promised them.

In one of the suit-cases which had been opened for the twins' mother to get out heavy coats and sweaters, Flossie found her big doll. She had insisted that "Babs", as she called her, must go to Eskimo Land. Finally, Mr. Bobbsey had consented.

Flossie now took out her "baby", sorry for having forgotten her so long. She fussed over the big doll, putting on its heavy coat and winding a muffler tightly about its throat.

"I don't want her to catch cold," she said to Freddie.

Her twin was inclined to be a little disgusted by all this fussing.

"It's only a doll," he said. "How can a doll feel cold?"

His sister was not to be stopped in her playing.

"Babs is my baby," said Flossie firmly, "and I am her mother. So you see, I have to keep her warm."

At last came the day when the Bobbseys and Miss Lamson were to leave the train and board a Hudson Bay steamer which was to take them on the next part of their trip to Cold Star. There was a good deal of hustle and bustle everywhere as they got on the boat. In the excitement, "Babs" was pushed from Flossie's arms and swept overboard.

"Oh, my baby!" cried the little girl wildly. "My baby has fallen into the water!"

CHAPTER VIII

A BRAVE RESCUE

"OH, my poor baby," wailed Flossie desperately. "Please, someone, save my poor baby!"

Now, it so happened that a deck-hand, a husky young fellow with a frank, open face, had been standing quite close to the Bobbseys as they went on board the steamer.

At Flossie's cry he had turned swiftly, had seen something white, apparently a baby, hurtle over the gang-plank and fall with a splash.

"She's in the deep water!" cried Flossie. "A fish might eat her!"

In another moment the young sailor had jumped overboard, diving straight for the spot where Flossie's big doll had disappeared.

Everyone rushed to the rail of the steamer to see what was happening.

In a moment the sailor reappeared, sputtering and blowing. In his hand he gripped a doll.

"Flossie!" Mrs. Bobbsey had the little girl by the shoulder and was shaking her gently. "Do you mean to say that brave young man dived down there so gallantly just to get your—doll?"

"Well, I dropped her, Mother," Flossie explained. "I just couldn't let her drown."

"Oh, dear," said Mrs. Bobbsey. "Whatever can I say to that poor young man?"

The brave seaman had pulled himself up on to the gang-plank, with the big doll gripped in one powerful fist. Mrs. Bobbsey approached him, looking dreadfully embarrassed.

"I'm so sorry," she said. "I would have stopped you if I had known in time that it was only my little girl's doll that had fallen overboard."

"That's all right, ma'am," said the man with a good-natured grin. "The little girl didn't know any better. Kids do set a lot of store by their dolls, no mistake."

The young man refused Mr. Bobbsey's offer of a reward, saying that what he had done was "all in the day's work".

The other passengers seemed very much amused by the incident. Friendly smiles greeted the Bobbseys on all sides as they went to their cabins.

"My poor baby is all wet," mourned Flossie, holding the dripping doll away from her. "It will be a wonder if she doesn't catch her death of cold."

"It will be a wonder if that poor young seaman doesn't catch *his* death of cold," worried Mrs. Bobbsey. "We must find out who he is, Richard," she added to her husband, "and reward him."

"I will," Mr. Bobbsey promised. "I'll speak to the captain as soon as I get you all settled, and find out the name of our hero. Perhaps we can do something for his family, even if he refuses to accept a reward for himself."

Mr. Bobbsey was as good as his word. When he had made certain that his family were settled in the three comfortable state-rooms reserved for them, he went in search of the captain.

"The man's name is Martin Shay," said the skipper. "He is a fine fellow and an able seaman, none better. He is married to a very sweet lady, and has two young children, a boy and a girl. The girl," reflected the officer, "must be about the same age as your little Flossie. The boy is a fine, manly little fellow, who looks very much like his father.

"Shay carries pictures of his kiddies with him wherever he goes," said Captain Berry with a warm smile. "It's really a sort of joke among his shipmates, the way he acts about them. But I don't blame him. They are great youngsters."

Mr. Bobbsey thanked the captain and returned to his family. When he gave them the information he had learned about Martin Shay, they tried to think up some way whereby they might thank the young man without appearing to force themselves upon him.

It was Flossie who had the real inspiration. "I could dress a doll for his little girl," she said. "Perhaps Martin Shay would like that."

"I am quite sure his child would, at any rate," said Mrs. Bobbsey, smiling. "I think that would be a very good idea, Flossie. I am sure Nan will give you any help you may need in dressing the doll."

"Of course I will. But where are we to get one?" asked Nan.

It appeared that Flossie had an answer all ready for this question too. Importantly she beckoned to Nan.

"I'll show you," said the little girl.

Her chubby hands reached beneath the clothes

which she had brought along for her favourite baby, and finally drew forth a small china doll.

"She doesn't look very pretty with only a nightie on," Flossie apologized. "But I brought some things to dress her in. Look!"

Before Nan's delighted eyes Flossie showed a rainbow collection of dress remnants, odds and ends of materials that Mrs. Bobbsey had handed over to Flossie at various times. The little girl had evidently put them into a suit-case when the family were packing for the trip.

There was a piece of bright red material from one of Flossie's own dresses, a bit of plaid cloth from a skirt belonging to Nan, and a lot of white flannel from some last summer's sports clothes.

"We can make a white coat and bonnet for the doll," planned Nan delightedly. "And a pair of white mittens, perhaps."

"A red dress would be pretty," added Flossie. "And there is ever so much nice cloth for petticoats and panties!"

Thus supplied, the sisters set to work very happily. Soon there were scraps of red and white and plaid material everywhere, while needles, spools of thread, and bits of lace were scattered about the state-room in wild confusion.

Meanwhile, Bert had made friends with one of the boatmen and the lad was being allowed to inspect a wireless set in the room above the deck. He listened to the *tap-tap-tap* as the operator heard the incoming signals.

"It must be lots of fun to get messages," said the

Bobbsey boy, "and when I am older I'm going to build a sending set in my home."

"That's fine," answered the man. "I began that way when I was a child. All the kids in my neighbourhood were crazy to help me—we formed a club, and it was a great success."

"You have given me a real idea," exclaimed Bert, "and when I get back to Lakeport I'll talk it over with my chums."

"Lakeport, did you say?" asked Jack Tripp, the operator. "Well, that's just the town where I was born."

"Gee! Isn't it funny," laughed Bert, "to meet you way up here?"

Suddenly there came a sound which interrupted further conversation.

Tap! Tap! Tap!

"Strange I can't make any sense of this message," muttered Tripp in a puzzled way.

" 'Ate a bat'—no sense to that."

Tap-Tap-Tap-Tap.

" 'Boot cat.' "

"Something's wrong here," growled Jack, beginning to tighten several screws and wires.

"Oh! Look!" cried Bert. "My little brother. He's outside the door. Come in, Freddie. How did you get here?"

"I followed you," explained the little fellow. "I like it up in this place."

No more queer noises were heard. Suddenly Jack Tripp said to Freddie, "Were you rapping, by any chance?"

"Well," said the small boy, "I thought I'd try tapping and tapping on the lock. It made a nice tune. See! *Clicky-Clicky—Click!*"

The man burst into a hearty roar. "So you were the 'bat and boot'. That *was* a good joke on me."

Bert joined in the laughter, and then took his brother back to the deck. It was then that the two boys learned of the surprise that was to take place on the ship that evening.

"I'll run down to the state-room," cried Freddie, "and tell the girls. I bet they don't know the news."

"All right," said Bert.

The girls' activity was interrupted by Freddie.

"There's going to be a party in the dining-room," said the little boy importantly, "with paper caps, and balloons, and everything."

Naturally, Nan and Flossie hurried to dress when they heard this, for they were excited at the thought of going to a real party on a ship. The dining-salon of the steamer was not large, but it was cheery and there was a festive air about the place.

In the centre of each table, with its snowy cloth, was a bouquet of artificial flowers, so cleverly made as to seem real. At each place there was a brightly coloured paper cap, and a small basket containing nuts and coloured candies.

At the door of the dining-room stood a steward. As each passenger entered he gave out a stick, at the end of which was fastened an enormous, bright-coloured balloon.

Everything was very gay and beautiful. People who were total strangers nodded and smiled at one another. Freddie and Flossie got the giggles when they saw Daddy Bobbsey marching up the room, holding his balloon over his shoulder for all the world as if it were a gun.

Miss Lamson was greeted several times by acquaintances as she accompanied the Bobbseys to the captain's table where their places were.

"What a lot of people you seem to know, Miss Lamson," remarked Bert, as they took their places. "Is everyone a friend of yours?"

"Not quite everyone," smiled the teacher. "Some of these people are going to Cold Star, others are bound for settlements still farther north. A great many of them I don't know at all," she added.

"Captain Berry, you make lots of trips to this country. Have you ever heard of a man named Harry Weller?" asked Mr. Bobbsey.

"No," said the captain. He paused for a moment, then asked, "Are you trying to find him?"

"Yes," replied Mr. Bobbsey. "My reason for wanting to locate Mr. Weller is to hand over to him a fortune left to him by his uncle, who has died. If I don't find him by a certain time, he'll lose it. The last word we had from Weller came to us from the neighbourhood of Cold Star settlement. That is why I am going there."

"What an interesting story!" said the captain. 'I hope you find your man, Mr. Bobbsey. You may be sure I will do all in my power to aid you."

The twins enjoyed a delicious dinner. Later on there was a marionette show and other games especially arranged for the entertainment of the children on board. Everybody put on paper caps, and the little folks laughed loud and long at mothers and fathers, professors and dignified teachers, their heads topped with dunce caps, high head-dresses, or the kind of bonnet with bells on that clowns in the circus wear.

Flossie and Freddie had so much fun that they pouted a little when Mrs. Bobbsey said it was time for all good little boys and girls to go to bed.

"We are having such a grand evening," said Flossie.

"I guess I never laughed so much before in my life," said Freddie. "Golly, everybody looked awfully funny!"

Next morning the children were up bright and early. Bundled in their heaviest clothing, they ran about the deck or leaned against the ship's rail, eagerly gazing upon the bleak shore-line. The scenery, so different from anything they had ever seen before, fascinated them. Cold as it was, they loved it, because it spoke to them of the mystery and secrets of the great North country.

Here and there a group of wooden shacks dotted the landscape. Once Freddie saw in the far distance a trapper driving a dog team.

"I don't see any igloos," complained Flossie.

"I expect the igloos are farther inland," said Nan. "We will probably see plenty of them when we get to Cold Star."

During the morning Flossie and Nan left the deck long enough to finish dressing the doll for Martin Shay's little girl.

Finally the new "baby" was all ready, even to a white cap and tiny white mittens. Flossie put her very carefully in a box which Nan had lined with tissue-paper, and covered her over with an another layer of it "so she wouldn't get cold".

This done, the two sisters went in search of Martin Shay.

The young man was in the act of scrubbing part of the after-deck. He blushed a brick-red when Flossie explained their errand to him. Nan noticed that he sent rather a sheepish look at a group of grinning deck-hands who were looking on.

He was very nice about the gift, however, and thanked the girls again and again for it, promising to have his own little girl write them a note of thanks as soon as he should reach home with the lovely doll. He even showed Nan and Flossie a picture of his daughter.

A short time after their talk with Martin Shay, Freddie brought his sisters some exciting news. The steamer, he said, was to stop for supplies a little farther down the shore.

'We can go on land if we want to," said Freddie. "Mother says we are to wear our overshoes."

"I think we are getting to shore already," said Nan.

"Oh, let's hurry!" cried Flossie.

The twins rushed below for their overshoes, and returned just as the steamer touched the dock. Eagerly they scanned the scene.

The settlement, as viewed from the ship, seemed to be a fairly large one. Groups of one-story frame buildings extended for some distance inland. At the shore-line an odd group, made up of white traders, Eskimos, and Indians, had gathered to greet the steamer.

The first thing Bert saw when he set foot on land was an Eskimo, who carried over one arm a basketful of the most adorable puppies he had ever seen. He wanted one at once and rushed over to the owner of the little dogs. Without warning, the mother of the animals, mistaking the Bobbsey boy's excitement, made a swift leap for Bert's throat.

CHAPTER IX

THE ESKIMO DOG

FOR a moment the lad from Lakeport seemed in great danger, but a passing stranger with a harpoon shoved the beast aside. Soon the Eskimo owner made the dog understand the boy was friendly.

Then the entire Bobbsey family gathered about the basketful of puppies, which were very cute and fat. They had beautiful little faces and sharp, pointed noses, and were covered all over with a thick, silky down like rabbit fur. They kept trying to climb out of the basket, but each time they did so they would fall back again with a foolish look of surprise that sent the children into gales of laughter.

"Aren't they sweet!" cried Nan. "Daddy, please buy us one!"

"Yes, Daddy, please do!" begged Flossie.

The Eskimo holding the basket grinned broadly and showed two rows of strong, white teeth.

"Very nice Eskimo dog," he said, pointing to the puppies. "Make very nice grown-up dog some day."

Mr. Bobbsey looked at Mrs. Bobbsey, his hand half-way to his pocket.

For a long moment, or so it seemed to the Bobbsey

twins, Mrs. Bobbsey hesitated. Then she nodded and smiled.

"I think we should," she said. "The puppies really are adorable, and the children never will be satisfied until they get one."

Then there followed the exciting task of picking out a puppy to be their very own. It was Bert who finally selected a fat little black and white fellow with perfect markings and roly-poly walk.

"But he's going to be partly ours, Bert, even if you did pick him out," said Freddie.

"Oh, sure," Bert grinned. "I'll let you play with him now and then."

Most of the Eskimos had things to sell, but the twins were so excited over their puppy they had eyes for scarcely anything else.

As they were returning to the steamer they came across an Indian who had long dog-whips for sale. Freddie wanted one of them, and Mr. Bobbsey let him have one, warning him, at the same time, to be careful how he used it.

Freddie said he would be very careful indeed, and a few minutes later the Bobbsey party returned to the boat. When they got there they found that most of the passengers had already arrived.

Mr. and Mrs. Bobbsey went to join a group of friends who were talking to Miss Lamson. The children, however, stood at the rail to watch the gang-plank as it was being drawn up, and also to show what they had bought to a group of youngsters.

The puppy, of course, was the main attraction. Everyone who pressed forward said how cute it was, and patted the silken head. No one even bothered to look at Freddie's nice new whip.

Perhaps the little boy grew tired of not being noticed at all, and thought that it was time for somebody to do something different, and not play with the little puppy all the time. At any rate, he stepped back from the group, and with a loud whoop swung the dog-whip about his head.

"Look what I have!" he shouted.

The group about Bert and the Eskimo puppy turned around. They were just in time to see the little boy bring the stout lash down with a crack.

It was unfortunate for both Freddie and Captain Berry that the latter happened to walk directly in the path of the whip. As it was, it flicked the legs of the captain very sharply indeed.

Freddie gave a startled cry. Captain Berry whirled about, his face red with anger. The little twin thought he had never before seen anyone look quite so furious.

"Who did that?" cried the captain. He saw Freddie with the whip in his hand and took an angry step towards him. "You young rascal! I've a good mind to teach you a lesson!"

"I didn't mean to do it, Captain Berry. Honest, I didn't," gasped Freddie. "I guess the whip just— sort of—slipped——"

"Go to your state-room, Freddie!" said Mr. Bobbsey. His face was stern, and his son guessed that he must be very angry. "Go to your room and stay there until I come to you. But first give me that dog-lash."

As the little lad turned away, he heard his father apologize to Captain Berry and heard the skipper's gruff reply.

Freddie found the lonely state-room and sat down stiffly in a chair. He had to fight to keep back the tears. It was bad enough, he thought, to be in disgrace with Daddy, but to have his precious dog-whip taken from him was almost more than he could bear.

For what seemed hours he sat there all alone. When at last he heard footsteps in the corridor and saw the door open, the little boy fairly flung himself across the room.

"I'm so sorry, Daddy," he cried in a tearful voice. "I didn't mean to do it. I wouldn't hurt the captain. I like him. And please, may I have my dog-whip again?"

"When you can learn to use it properly," said Mr. Bobbsey gravely. "Come over here, Freddie. I want to talk to you."

Mr. Bobbsey sat on the edge of the bed. He put his arm about his son and spoke to him for some time. When he had finished, Freddie promised to be more careful and thoughtful of other people.

"Do you suppose we could find Captain Berry?" he asked. "I'd like to tell him I'm sorry."

Mr. Bobbsey got up. He smiled and looked at his watch. "I think you'll just have time before luncheon," he said.

The rest of the trip to Cold Star, though not at all exciting, passed very pleasantly. Mr. Bobbsey made friends with all the passengers, because he hoped to find out something that would help him in his search for Harry Weller. As yet no useful information had turned up, but Mr. Bobbsey was sure that he would meet someone at Cold Star who might be able to tell him about the man.

Meanwhile, the Eskimo puppy thrived and was the delight and pet of all on board. Flossie had named the little fellow "Igloo", and the name stuck in spite of Bert's protest that it was ridiculous to name a dog after a house.

When they were only a few hours' journey from Cold Star an aeroplane swooped down over the steamer with a startling roar. It came so close that the children ducked their heads. As they did so, a small object struck the deck in front of them, rolled for a short distance, and then came to rest directly at Nan's feet.

"My! Where did that come from?" cried Flossie.

"Someone in the aeroplane must have dropped it," said Freddie in huge excitement. "That's why it came so near our boat."

Bert rushed up as Nan was unwrapping the mysterious packet.

"Whew! that aeroplane came close," he exclaimed, squinting at the disappearing plane. "Seemed as though the pilot wanted to make a landing on deck. What have you there, Nan?"

"It's a letter," the girl discovered. "All done up in a waterproof wrapper!"

"The aeroplane dropped it," Freddie explained, peering over his sister's arm to get a glimpse of the letter. "What does it say, Nan?"

"It's addressed to Miss Helen Lamson, and way

down in the left-hand corner of the envelope is the word 'personal'. I wonder who could have sent it."

"Might be a good idea to look for Miss Lamson and find out," suggested Bert.

The young lady was in the cabin she shared with Nan and Flossie. She looked up with a smile as the children entered. When they gave her the letter and explained how they got it, the teacher at first seemed surprised; then a pleased look came over her face as her eyes dropped to the writing on the envelope.

"It's from Al Faber," she exclaimed. "How like him to send me a message this way! Don't go," she added, as the children turned away politely. "I'll read what he has to say and tell you about it, if you like."

As this was just what the twins had hoped for, they waited gladly, watching closely while Miss Lamson turned page after page of the bulky letter. It seemed to Flossie that the teacher looked more and more pleased the longer she read. Nan could not help but notice that the flush on her face made her look almost beautiful.

At last the settlement worker finished reading the letter. She folded it and smiled at the children.

"All good news," she told them. "Mr. Faber says his plane has been repaired and is almost ready for flight again. He will reach Cold Star only a short time after we do."

"We are almost at Cold Star now, aren't we?" asked Nan.

"Yes. We will land very soon, and journey the rest of the way to the settlement by sled."

"Dog sled?" demanded Freddie eagerly.

Miss Lamson nodded, smiling at his enthusiasm.

"I've sent word ahead to have them ready for us."

"Golly!" cried Freddie happily. "I hope we land right away!"

At last the moment came when they stood by the deck rail waiting to go ashore. Suit-cases were neatly packed and strapped. Igloo, nestled in a bag Nan had made for him and from which only his shaggy, rumpled head stuck out, whined and squirmed beneath Bert's arm. Mr. and Mrs. Bobbsey and Miss Lamson were bundled up to their eyes in heavy wraps for the temperature had gone down and now it was bitterly cold. The twins wound their snug mufflers tighter about their throats, and stamped their feet to keep them warm.

Then the gangplank was lowered and last good-byes were said to Captain Berry and the few passenger still aboard the steamer. Flossie waved to Martin Shay, the seaman, who had come to see them off, and waited shyly in the background.

At last they were ashore. They stood on the hard, desolate coast, their baggage grouped about them, while the gangplank was pulled up. Then the steamer moved off slowly through the ice-clogged waters.

As the Bobbsey party turned away, Flossie suddenly lifted her face skywards. Something small and soft, light as a feather, but very cold, touched her cheek.

"It's beginning to snow," she said.

"Then we must be off at once." Miss Lamson looked anxiously at the dark sky. "It will never do for us to be caught in a blizzard before we reach Cold Star."

The dogsleds were waiting. There were three of them, and all were roomy enough to take care of the Bobbseys, Miss Lamson, and their luggage. Harnessed to each sled, and straining to be off, were six beautiful huskies and a lead dog.

Freddie and Flossie wanted to stop and pet the huskies, but Miss Lamson hurried them on.

"We must reach Cold Star before the snow gets too bad," she said.

Three strapping Eskimos, native to the region, had charge of the dog teams. To them Miss Lamson spoke in their native tongue. They set to work at once packing the luggage and getting the group comfortably settled.

"We'll race your team," cried Freddie eagerly to his brother.

"All right," responded Bert happily, as he admired the straining dogs fastened to his sled.

It was arranged that the teacher was to travel with the luggage in the first sled. Mrs. Bobbsey would go with Nan and Bert in the second one, while Mr. Bobbsey would bring up the rear with the two small twins.

Long, snake-like whips cracked in the brittle air, the drivers shouted, the sleds lurched forward. They were off!

CHAPTER X

AT COLD STAR

NOTHING could ever equal the thrill and delight the twins felt on that ride in a dogsled. The bitter wind whipped against their faces, but this did not worry them, for they were warm and snug beneath furry laprobes.

Down snow-covered hills they raced, the dogs galloping ahead, sending forth sprays of ice and snow from their flying feet. Again the way would lead uphill, when the dogs had to work harder. Then the Eskimo drivers would run with them, urging them on with loud cries. At these times Freddie would ask to get out and walk to lighten the load, but Mr. Bobbsey forbade him. He explained that his weight scarcely mattered to the powerful beasts.

They had covered perhaps half the distance to Cold Star, when another dog team appeared on the horizon, sharply outlined against the dark sky. The sled was scarcely more than a dot at first, but it grew rapidly larger as it bore down upon them.

Suddenly Freddie shouted with glee.

"Look, Daddy, they are trappers, and their sled is loaded with furs!"

Mr. Bobbsey called to the Eskimo runner to stop.

The native brought the dogs to a standstill as the other sled drew up to them.

The children's daddy motioned to the fur-clad trappers. "We'd like some of your pelts if you don't ask too much for them," he said.

At once the men smiled. They told Mr. Bobbsey that he would find no prices as reasonable as theirs anywhere in the North country.

Rather to Mr. Bobbsey's surprise, this seemed to be true. The pelts were so inexpensive that Freddie and Flossie were allowed to choose the ones they liked best, not only for themselves, but for Nan and Bert as well. These would later be made into wraps and fur hoods for the children, to keep them warm even in the bitter cold climate of Eskimo Land.

Before they went on their way Mr. Bobbsey asked the trappers if they had ever heard of a man named Harry Weller. The men smiled, then spread their hands out in a helpless gesture.

"Perhaps," said one. "Who can tell?"

Half an hour later they reached the settlement. They came upon it suddenly as their path led them around a pile of snow-covered rocks which had hidden it from view.

The place was made up of half a dozen rambling frame buildings. They were snow-covered, and were grouped in a sort of circle. They looked very lovely, set as they were in that waste of ice and snow.

However, as the children came nearer they could see lights winking from some of the windows. Suddenly a door opened and several people came out.

They stood in the snow, eagerly waiting to welcome the group of travellers.

Miss Lamson stepped from the leading sled. She spoke to various members of the group, then turned around to welcome the Bobbseys as they came up towards the settlement.

"These are all my good friends," she told them gravely. She placed her hand on the head of a sturdy Eskimo standing next to her, and slipped her arm about the shoulders of a native boy. "I shall not introduce them all to you now because I know you are hungry and tired.

"First you must get warm and have something to eat. But if you are going to stay with us at the settlement I know it won't be long before you will learn to regard all these people as your friends, and to trust them as I do."

The Eskimos broke into a flood of welcoming speech in their native tongue. Miss Lamson answered them in their language, at the same time telling them to go back to the low, shed-like structure they had just left. The Bobbseys followed them, and when they got to the building they looked about it with great curiosity.

The room was long and low, and it seemed very hot after the bitter cold of the journey. The place was not uncomfortable, although it was crowded with furniture and books. Papers were strewn about everywhere. There were prints on the walls and Indian rugs on the rough floor. At one end of the room stood a large couch covered by a red and white rug, and heaped high with gay-coloured pillows.

"Our people have made almost everything in this room," Miss Lamson explained, smiling. "The rugs, the cushions, the book-shelves, even some of the furniture are their work. They are very willing and want to work; intelligent, and learn easily if properly taught."

Miss Lamson showed the Bobbseys several other rooms, including the kitchen and the bare but cheerful dining-room. Here, Miss Lamson explained, the Bobbsey family would take their meals with the teacher and her staff.

"Your sleeping quarters are in another building which is connected by a passage with this one," she said. "You see, you won't have to go out-of-doors to get to your bedrooms."

The twins thought it was great fun to walk through the passage with its low roof. The walls were so close together that there was scarcely room enough for Daddy Bobbsey's broad shoulders to pass through.

The bedrooms were small but comfortably furnished, each having a chest of drawers, a double bed, two chairs, and a washstand with a basin and pitcher. On a shelf stood two fat tallow candles set in deer-horn holders.

"Won't it be fun to dress by candlelight?" cried Flossie excitedly.

"Everything is thrilling about this place," said Nan happily. "I love it!"

After a while a young Eskimo came to tell them that dinner was ready. The boy's name was Puk, and he was very shy with the strange white children. When they tried to talk to him he would hang his head and turn away so that they gave up trying.

"He will make friends with us later," Bert said, "when he comes to know us better."

In the dining-room Miss Lamson introduced the Bobbsey family to the members of her staff. There were the two Talley sisters, both teachers; the nurse, who was a red-haired, plump-faced woman who smiled at the twins; and Doctor Bramley, the settlement physician.

"So you are going to be an Eskimo?" laughed the doctor as he pinched Flossie's rosy cheeks.

"Yes, Doctor, I used to be Daddy's fat fairy, but now I think I'll be an Eskimo teacher."

"Oho," cried the man, "we have a real helper here."

"I'm going to be a trapper," exclaimed Freddie, not to be outdone by his sister.

As for Mrs. Bobbsey and the older twins, they were interested in everyone and everything. They listened while the Misses Talley and the pleasant nurse told of their work among the natives. Then they all tasted the hot, thick soup served by an Eskimo woman, Anak, and thought it was very good. They watched the boy Puk as he walked shyly about the table, helping Anak.

"I think we'll like it here," whispered Bert to Nan, "even if it is so different from home."

After dinner they went into the recreation hall. Miss Lamson called Puk aside and told him to go to her room and bring back the two suit-cases he would find there. "I have a surprise in there for all of you," she said.

When the boy returned, a travelling bag in each

hand, Miss Lamson called all her "people" to her. They came, crowding into the long room. Each wore a broad smile.

"Bigee party," laughed Anak. "Miss Lamson good. Glad she back."

The teacher had something for everyone. For the women there were yards of bright-coloured calico-cloth and strings of beads. For the men she had felt slippers, woollen socks and thick, warm sweaters. The children received toys. The music-box fell to the lot of a little Eskimo girl named Nyla.

"I'll show you how to play it," said Freddie, pointing to the little gift. "May I?"

The dark-haired girl nodded.

Puk was given a baseball bat and a ball and catcher's glove, at which he stared with solemn, puzzled eyes. The gun, the fire-engine and numerous pretty toys fell to the lot of other children of the settlement.

Miss Lamson had not forgotten the people who worked with her. When she had handed out all the packages, everyone felt happy. The two Talley ladies each had several yards of fine wool for dresses. Miss Waters, the nurse, received a pair of furry, wool-lined mittens and a special type of nurses' bag which could be used when she went on trips to other parts of Eskimo Land.

"May I look inside it?" asked Flossie.

"Of course," said the lady. "Maybe some day you can help me carry it on an important case."

Dr. Bramley lovingly examined a delicate surgical instrument he had needed for a long time, and which could not be bought any place but in the United States.

"No wonder everybody at the settlement adores Miss Lamson," thought Nan. "How kind she is, and how much she does for everybody!"

In the course of his rambles about the room Bert found himself beside Puk. The lad was still holding the baseball bat. He turned it over and over in his hands with the same puzzled stare as before.

"I'll show you how to use it tomorrow, if you like," Bert offered.

The Eskimo boy looked at the Bobbsey lad's smiling face, then his glance fell upon the bat again. After a moment he said with a shy smile, "Me like!"

That was the beginning of a firm friendship between Puk and the Bobbsey twins.

Mr. Bobbsey had been questioning Doctor Bramley and several natives about his lost friend, Harry Weller. He believed he had a valuable clue. But it was not until the next morning that the children learned the story.

Hurriedly Mr. Bobbsey kissed his family good-bye. Then Mrs. Bobbsey told of his forthcoming search for his friend.

"Doctor Bramley," she explained, "believes Mr. Weller has gone North to explore. A man who looked like him was seen by the natives to pass through here many, many months ago."

"Will it be dangerous for Daddy to go up there?" asked Nan seriously.

"Well, we hope the trip will be over before bad weather sets in."

After breakfast the children bundled themselves into their heaviest clothing and hurried out, accompanied by the fat Eskimo puppy Igloo, to see what Cold Star looked like by daylight.

Puk and Nyla, the two Eskimo children, wore parkas. This was the native outdoor dress of the region, a garment half cape and half coat, and made of fur with an attached pointed hood also of fur.

Puk carried the bat and ball. He looked at Bert eagerly, for he remembered that the friendly boy had said he would show him how to use the wonderful new toy.

Bert was as good as his word. He picked his team, marking out a field in the snow, and decided he would stand at bat. Nan was pitcher, while Freddie stationed himself behind the batter to catch any balls Bert might not hit.

Flossie, who was not very good as a baseball player, was given a position as outfielder. Puk and Nyla agreed just to stand aside and watch until they should become familiar with the game.

Everything went on merrily. Bert made several home runs. Freddie shouted with glee at Nan's funny pitching. Puk and Nyla forgot to be shy. In fact, everyone was having so much fun that it was a long time before they discovered that Flossie had disappeared.

CHAPTER XI

THE DESERTED VILLAGE

IT was hard for the children to believe at first that Flossie had gone very far away. They searched for her everywhere, calling her name loudly.

Nan thought that Flossie might perhaps have gone back into the house for something. Freddie said that he was sure she hadn't because he had been near the door all the time and would have been certain to have seen his sister if she had passed that way.

"Well, then, where can she be?" cried Nan.

"She might be hiding," said Freddie.

The children, guided by Puk and Nyla, searched the other buildings of the settlement. They looked every place they could think of, but still could find no sign of Flossie.

Bert said they ought to tell their mother, but Nan thought it would be too bad to frighten Mrs Bobbsey, especially since Flossie was certain to appear very soon.

"Flossie!" shouted Bert. "Where are you?"

There was no answer.

"Are you hurt?" called Nan excitedly.

Still there was no response.

Freddie tried hard to whistle for his twin, but soon gave it up.

"Maybe she got eaten up by a bear," suggested the little boy in fright.

When Freddie said bear, Bert turned to Puk but that lad shook his head as if to say "No".

Bert wished his father had not gone away to search for Mr. Weller quite so soon. If Flossie were really lost Mr. Bobbsey should be told, he felt. His father would know what to do and where to look for the little girl.

Now Nyla spoke in broken English, very shyly and haltingly. "One more place to look," she said. "Come."

She led the wondering children to a snow-topped knoll, and pointed.

"Strange Eskimo lived there—one time," she said, pointing to several huts in the distance. "Gone now."

At her words Nan clapped her hands. She turned to Nyla eagerly.

"You mean the Eskimos were here at one time but have gone away. When they went they deserted their homes. But why should Flossie go there?"

Nyla smiled, and shrugged her shoulders.

"Some old igloos! I bet we'll find Flossie there!" cried Bert. "Let's go!"

Slipping, sliding, clutching at one another wildly, the children ran down the icy slope, led by the fleet-footed Puk and Nyla. At their heels raced the Bobbsey puppy, barking in short baby yaps and tripping over himself in an effort to keep up with them.

"Flossie! Flossie!"

Soon they came to the outskirts of what had once been a small Eskimo village. They looked with interest in the empty huts.

A few broken objects were lying about. At one spot, which had no doubt once been a sort of village dumping ground, was a heap of bones, the remains of a few pieces of fur, and some other refuse. At the entrance to the village two poles stood upright. From a wire strung between them a few scraps of dried meat still dangled.

The children looked about them with interest. They would have enjoyed seeing all this very much if they had not been so eager to find Flossie.

"What funny looking meat," said Freddie, wrinkling up his nose. "I'd hate to have to eat it."

Suddenly Puk pointed to the little dog, Igloo.

"Look! Puppy very smart dog. He know something!"

The Bobbsey pet was indeed acting very strangely. He had his funny little nose to the ground and was wabbling about on his short, fat legs.

"He's getting Flossie's scent," shouted Freddie. "I bet he knows where she is."

As though he wanted to show Freddie he knew what he meant, the dog paused at the entrance to an unused hut. He yapped once, then waddled on his short legs through the opening.

"Golly, I bet he's found Flossie. I bet he has," cried Freddie.

Sure enough, when the children crowded to the door of the old igloo they found Flossie inside, sitting on a dirty fur pelt full of holes. She had found a wooden platter, two half-burned tallow candles, a battered iron spoon, and a string of bright red beads. She looked very happy.

"Oh, Flossie, how could you worry us so?" cried Nan. "We thought you were lost."

"Come on in," Flossie invited. "I've found loads and loads of the loveliest things. I'm playing Eskimo."

"You gave us an awful scare," Bert grumbled. "You'd better come home now. It must be almost time for lunch."

"And Mother will be worried," Nan added.

It was hard to get Flossie away from her new playthings. It was only by promising to let her come to the village again very soon that they were able to get her to return with them to the settlement.

On the way back Flossie carried Igloo. The puppy's short legs were tired and he snuggled up gratefully against the little girl's woolly coat. Puk reached up shyly and stroked the dog's shaggy head.

"Him nice dog. Him smart," said Puk.

In the days that followed the friendship between Puk and Nyla and the Bobbsey twins grew stronger and stronger. Through the two Eskimos the children came to know the country around Cold Star as they never could have done alone.

In company with Puk and Nyla they visited several neighbouring villages. The natives were always friendly. They told the children in broken English stories of their hunts for the polar bear and the walrus and showed them the long, sharp-pointed spears which they had learned to throw without ever missing. Sometimes they gave the visitors food, placing in the hands bowls of steaming stew which had fat and pieces of seal meat floating about in it.

The children liked the food all right, but they had to refuse when they were offered chunks of half-cooked bear or walrus meat still sizzling from the fire and oozing fat.

"What awful meat," said Flossie on one such occasion. "Mine is almost raw."

"Lots of the Eskimos eat their meat without cooking it at all," explained Bert, lowering his voice. "That's what their name means, you know—eater of raw meat."

"Well, they can have it. I like mine cooked," Nan said, though she was very careful, of course, not to say it so the Eskimos could hear her.

Meanwhile, Mr. Bobbsey continued the search for the missing Mr. Weller. One day, upon returning with the native hunters, he brought along a seal which he had helped to kill. He had found out a few things about Mr. Weller, he said, and felt sure he would find him before very long.

Anak had made parkas for all the children from the pelts Mr. Bobbsey had bought on the way to the settlement. The furs were very nice and warm. The twins could stay out for hours now in the freezing air without feeling any discomfort from the cold.

One day Freddie noticed that there was something wrong with Igloo's foot. The little dog walked with a limp, and when Freddie picked up its paw to examine it, the puppy whined and licked the little boy's hand.

Without saying anything, Freddie made up his mind just what to do. In a neighbouring village there was an old shrivelled-up Eskimo named Looktoo. Looktoo was a sort of medicine man, who said he could cure anybody. He could certainly cure Igloo, thought Freddie.

Accordingly, with the puppy clutched tightly in his arms, Freddie set off for the Eskimo village. He found Looktoo in his hut, seated cross-legged on a bearskin rug. The man handled the puppy gently with his shrivelled, wrinkled hands.

"Sure, me fix him," he said.

While Freddie waited for his pet to be treated, he picked up an old bow which stood inside the door of the igloo. He fitted an arrow to it and drew it taut. Without meaning to do so, he let the arrow go. It winged past him with a singing sound and sped out through the door of the hut!

CHAPTER XII

GOOD LUCK

LOOKTOO jumped to his feet, jabbering angrily. He snatched the bow from Freddie's hand.

"No touch that!" he cried. "You hurt someone— maybe kill."

"I didn't mean to shoot it," Freddie said. "It just went off by itself."

Freddie's mistake seemed to have caused a great deal of excitement in the village. Two men who were hanging strips of meat to dry in front of their huts gave the alarm. Others poured out of igloos into the common meeting place. Some had weapons; others were empty-handed. All were excited and talking loudly.

"I wonder what can be the matter," said Freddie. "I hope the arrow didn't hit anyone. Golly, I wouldn't want to do that."

"Come. We see," said Looktoo.

As Freddie followed the medicine man out into the open air he was really very much afraid that he might have hurt someone by shooting the arrow off so carelessly.

He approached the crowd which had gathered on the big ice plateau at the edge of the village. His hand was clutched tightly in that of Looktoo.

The natives drew back to make room for the old man. Freddie was almost afraid to look at what he might see there. He closed his eyes for a second. When he opened them he saw that every one was grinning broadly. Even Looktoo was smiling. In the medicine man's hand a big bird dangled limply.

"You shoot him—with arrow," Looktoo explained. "Him strange bird. No see here—very much. Mean good luck."

Freddie was very happy to find that his careless action in shooting the arrow had brought good luck to his friends. He wondered how a dead gull could bring good luck, but he did not ask why. Looktoo was a wise man, thought little Freddie. He must surely know what he was talking about.

"Maybe it will bring good luck to my Daddy, too," he said, as he and Looktoo made their way back to the igloo. "Perhaps he will find Mr. Weller."

They reached the home of the medicine man, and Looktoo picked up the puppy. Very gently he pulled out a long, sharp splinter that had lodged in a tender part of the little dog's hind paw. For some time the medicine man did not speak. Then suddenly he looked at Freddie, his leathery face breaking into a thousand wrinkles.

"Your father—look for—man?" he asked. "His name—Weller? He—white man?"

"Yes," said Freddie eagerly. "Do you know him, Looktoo?"

For a long moment the Eskimo did not answer. Then he nodded.

"Me know man," he said. "White man—Weller—
good friend. Looktoo like."

Freddie understood by this that at some time in the
past Mr. Weller had helped Looktoo and his people.
Now Looktoo would tell nothing he knew about Mr.
Weller that might bring harm to his good friend.

Freddie hastened to explain to the old Eskimo that
his father was a friend of Mr. Weller also. "My
Daddy wants to give him some money," the little boy
said. "He wouldn't hurt him, Looktoo. He wouldn't
hurt anybody. He wants to make Mr. Weller happy."

"Humph!" Looktoo seemed to be thinking this
over. He finished dressing Igloo's foot and placed the
puppy on the ground. "Runner go long way off," he
said at last. "Come back. Say white man at place call
—White Hope."

"Oh, thank you very much, Looktoo," cried
Freddie. He could hardly wait to start back to the
settlement with his good news. "Is Igloo's foot all
right again, do you think?"

"Puppy—him fine," said Looktoo.

Freddie thanked the Eskimo again. He took the
dog in his arms and started out on the long walk to
Cold Star settlement. His family were becoming
worried about him. He told them about Igloo and the
reason for his visit to Looktoo.

Everyone made much of the dog. Flossie went out
to the kitchen to see if she could get a bit of raw
meat for the puppy. "Just to make him feel good
when he's having a sore foot," she said.

When Freddie told them what Looktoo had said
about Harry Weller, they were all delighted for

Daddy Bobbsey's sake. Mrs. Bobbsey went at once to see Miss Lamson about the best and quickest way to get word of this to her husband.

They decided to send a runner to find the children's father. He should act as Mr. Bobbsey's guide as far as the White Hope settlement.

One week, two weeks passed, and still there was no word from either the runner or Mr. Bobbsey. Those were anxious days for those waiting at Cold Star, especially when the early snows began to fall. Up to this time the weather had been fair except for the light flurry the day of the Bobbsey's arrival. The overcast sky and the light, steady fall of snow brought gloom to the hearts of the little group. Daddy Bobbsey was out in it somewhere, they knew.

As day followed day, and still there was no word from him, everyone grew more and more anxious. Mrs. Bobbsey began to spend most of her time at the window. The children were restless. The snow, which had always delighted them, now frightened them because it was just one more danger for their daddy to face.

When the strain became almost too great, the runner returned.

Nan was the first one to see him as he appeared over the ridge, a dark, moving blot against the white ground. At first she thought he might be her father; but a second look proved to her that this could not be so. Her daddy was with a party. This man was alone.

The runner brought good news. The family gathered in the big room at the settlement house to hear it and to ask the native many questions.

"Mr. Bobbsey, men with him, all safe," said the Eskimo. "They meet trappers Sakey and Joslind. These men mighty hunters. They go with white man and his party to White Hope."

Here Miss Lamson interrupted to explain that Sakey and Joslind were the trappers they had met the day of their arrival at Cold Star, and from whom Mr. Bobbsey had bought the furs for the children's parkas.

"They are both good men. They know every inch of this country," she told Mrs. Bobbsey. "Your husband will be safe with them."

"I hope so," said Mrs. Bobbsey anxiously. "But I do wish the snow would stop. It frightens me."

CHAPTER XIII

A SAVAGE FIGHT

ALTHOUGH the return of the Eskimo had somewhat reassured Mrs. Bobbsey and the twins as to Mr. Bobbseys' safety, they were still worried about him.

Miss Lamson had admitted a bit unwillingly, it seemed to them, that the settlement at White Hope could be reached only by a long and dangerous journey. It was far to the north where even Eskimo villages were rare. Anyone lost in that desolate region, the teacher was forced to say, would be in a very serious position indeed. As long as their food supply lasted they could keep going, of course. They would never be in danger of perishing from lack of water, as the snow could always be melted and drunk. Food was the most important item for them.

"But what is the sense in worrying about things that might never happen?" said Miss Lamson briskly. "Mr. Bobbsey will not get lost as long as Joslind and Sakey are with him. Probably he has already reached White Hope and will be back again with Mr. Weller before any of us realize it."

Meanwhile, things went on as usual at the settlement. Eskimos came for miles around, mushing over the snow with their handsome teams of huskies. In the classroom they hunched themselves over crude desks, patiently learning the secrets of the first primer. "I see a cat," they would read, "Does the cat love Nan?"

They brought their sick to the settlement to be treated by kind Doctor Bramley and the red-haired nurse. They took their troubles to Miss Lamson, who was always kind and helpful. Sometimes they would bring presents, and stand by, smiling happily when the teacher praised them. Everyone adored Miss Lamson.

One day a strange Eskimo mushed into the settlement, driving a fine team of huskies. However, when Freddie approached the handsome animals and was going to pat the lead dog on the head, the rough man warned him away very sharply.

"No touch," he said. "Wolf very wild dog. He bite little boy."

Indeed, the lead dog was well named. He was much more like a wolf than a dog, and would let no one but his master come near him. Then he would cringe as though afraid he would be struck. Freddie wondered if the man was cruel to the animal.

The little boy took a good look at the Eskimo and decided that he did not like his face at all. His eyes were cold and hard, like pieces of shiny black coal. His mouth looked as if he were mad. It somehow reminded Freddie of a trap, it was shut so tight and thin.

Just then Bert and Puk called to the little boy to come and have a snow fight. He joined them, and was so interested in making a snow fort that he forgot all about Nogasak, the Eskimo, and the dog called Wolf.

Some time later the children heard a wild growling and snarling in the settlement square. They knew there must be a terrible dog fight going on, and rushed back to see what was happening.

There were at least a dozen dogs in the battle, all barking and snapping viciously at one another. However, the object of their attack seemed to be a huge, greyish-white husky who fought like a mad beast.

"That's Nogasak's lead dog!" cried Freddie, jumping up and down in his excitement. "The big grey one. His name is Wolf."

People came running from the buildings. Suddenly Nogasak appeared. There was an ugly gleam in his eyes, and he carried a gun.

"Say, I hope that fellow doesn't shoot all the dogs!" cried Bert. "They're too valuable!"

The children ran down the slope towards the fighting animals. As they did so, they saw Nogasak raise his rifle. Before he could fire, another Eskimo had flung himself upon the cruel fellow. The gun went off into the air, and the dogs were not harmed.

Then the children saw a very brave thing. This same Eskimo who had kept Nogasak from shooting now plunged into the midst of the fighting dogs. He pushed and tugged at them, calling them by name and shouting commands at them. At any moment the animals could have turned upon him and torn him to pieces, but, bravely, he persisted in his efforts to separate the snarling beasts.

Other men of the settlement rushed to his aid. With dog whips, pleadings and threats, they finally managed to stop the terrible riot. The beasts drew away, snarling and licking their wounds.

Nogasak's husky hung about its master's heels. The big grey dog had suffered more serious injuries than had any of the others. He limped badly, and one torn ear dripped blood on to the white ground.

Anuk, the Eskimo who had risked death to separate the fighting dogs, came over to Nogasak.

"Your husky hurt bad," the children heard him say. "You take him to house. We fix."

The children saw Nogasak scowl as he put a hand on Wolf's fierce head.

"You no touch," said Nogasak sullenly. "You do harm enough. Wolf—I fix."

Anuk shrugged and turned away. Nogasak watched him for a moment, scowling; then went off to his own quarters with Wolf trailing at his heels.

"I don't like the looks of that new Eskimo," said Bert, as the children went back to their snow fight. "He's a wicked looking fellow, and that dog of his is a brute. I bet he'll make more trouble here before he moves on."

One morning, about two days after the battle of the settlement huskies with Nogasak's Wolf, Bert and Puk were passing through the kitchen. They came upon a pan of freshly-made, delicious-looking chocolate-looking fudge. It had a tempting odour.

Bert remembered that Nan had promised to teach Nyla how to make candy that morning. Putting two and two together, Bert decided that this panful was the result of a cooking lesson. Most likely the girls had left the fudge on the table to cool while they went off to do something else. Bert thought that Nan and Nyla would return soon, for a knife lay on the table ready to cut the fudge. A box, neatly lined with waxed paper, lay open to receive it.

The kitchen was empty at the moment. A feeling of mischief took hold of Bert, and he glanced from the pan of chocolates to Puk, then grinned.

"Let's hide the candy in the woodshed," he suggested. "When Nan and Nyla come back they'll think someone stole it. What do you say?"

Puk thought this would be great fun. He giggled delightedly as Bert carried the pan out to the little building in back. He watched with wide eyes as Bert placed pieces of wood before it so that it would be hidden entirely from the view of anyone entering the shed from the kitchen.

"They think someone take," chuckled Puk. "They be mad. Heap mad, maybe."

"Sh! I think they are coming," said Bert.

The boys just had time to hide in a small closet off the kitchen when Nan and Nyla entered.

"It must be cold now," they heard Nan say.

"Will taste good," said Nyla. "Very good."

The girls went straight to the table. There was a pause during which Bert looked through the crack of the closet door, and Puk tried to smother his laughter.

"Nyla! It's gone!" they heard Nan say. "Someone must have taken it. But who would be so mean as to do a thing like that, do you suppose?"

"Oh, nice candy," mourned Nyla. "All gone away. Someone take."

"Yes, and I'm going to find out *who* took it," said Nan, in the way she always spoke when she made up her mind to do something. "Whoever did is just too mean for——"

Here Nan broke off suddenly. Puk's mirth had exploded in a series of muffled giggles. She ran to the closet door and pushed it open. There stood the two guilty ones. Puk was holding his sides with laugher. Bert's face was one broad grin.

"So you did take our candy!" Nan accused them. "Now you come out here right away and tell us where you put it. Come on, now ! No more fooling!"

"Maybe they eat," said Nyla.

The idea that the two boys might have been able to eat the whole panful of candy in such a short time sent the boys into another outburst of mirth. Bert choked, he laughed so hard, and Nan had to pat him on the back.

"Oh, all right, you can have your candy," gasped Bert. "We only hid it in the woodshed."

Nan darted inside with Nyla close at her heels.

"Where is it?" she demanded. "I don't see it. I don't believe you put it there at all."

"Wait a minute—I'll show you."

Bert thrust himself past Nan and pushed aside the sticks of wood he had arranged to hide the pan of candy. Suddenly he paused and his face went blank, he was so startled. The shelf was bare. The candy, pan and all, had disappeared!

"Now what do you make of that!" cried Bert "I

put the fudge right there not five minutes ago. Puk saw me do it."

The Eskimo boy nodded. He pointed to the window above the shelf, and they saw it was now open, though Bert was sure it had been closed when he had placed the candy on the ledge.

"Window open," said Puk. "Someone stick in hand, steal candy. Go off with it."

"Maybe you're right," said Bert thoughtfully.

He looked out the window and was excited to see fresh tracks in the snow.

"If someone did steal it he can't be very far off. Look!" said Bert, pointing to the tracks.

Puk nodded.

"We run after thief. We find," said Puk.

Nan and Nyla watched the boys go. The girls had little faith that Bert and Puk could locate the person who had stolen their sweets. Meanwhile, they were very angry with the boys for the trick they had played on them.

"The next time we make a batch of candy they shan't have a piece, not a single piece," said Nan, as she closed the door. "I wish they had left our candy alone!"

"Nice candy," mourned Nyla. "Me like very, very much."

Meanwhile, Bert and Puk walked in the fresh tracks in the snow. The trail was easily followed, and led outwards in a direct line from the woodshed window to the shack where the huskies were tied.

Here the boys almost lost their way, for the route was crossed and re-crossed by other tracks that had been recently made. They picked it up, however, on the far side of the dog enclosure and followed it eagerly. They were excited now by the belief that they were close on the heels of the guilty person.

Puk paused suddenly, and pointed to a trail which met, at right angles, the one they were following.

"He meets the other man here," said Puk. "They go on together."

It was true that at this place the two trails joined and merged. The boys went more carefully, now that they knew they were on the path made by two men instead of one.

The double track led straight to the deserted village, and took them to the door of one of the old igloos, where it suddenly ended. At the same time the boys heard voices within the hut.

"Men here," muttered Puk. "We listen. Maybe hear something."

The boys bent down close to the opening. In clear tones they heard a voice they thought was Nogasak's say:

"I meet white man, three white man. They say 'Which is way to White Hope?' I tell them, but I tell them wrong. White man get lost, maybe. I think white man—maybe die."

CHAPTER XIV

THE BOY PUK

"WHITE man get lost, maybe. I think white man —maybe die."

Nogasak—if it was he—repeated the words with an ugly laugh. The person with him grunted, and Bert heard him say:

"You are bad man, Nogasak. White men get lost. Heavy snow come, they die for sure. You kill them."

"Good," returned Nogasak sullenly. "White man I hate. White man no good. Big snow come, they die. Good! White man's candy," said Nokasak after a brief pause, "him good."

"Yes," said his companion. "Candy good, very good."

Puk motioned to Bert. "Nogasak bad man," said the Eskimo lad softly. "We go back."

Bert agreed with Puk that little would be gained by going to Nogasak and accusing him of taking Nan's candy. The Eskimo would only laugh at them. There was nothing that the two boys could do by themselves to force him to give back the stolen sweets.

Besides, Bert had something far more important to worry about now. Nogasak had spoken of three white men who had asked the direction to White

Hope. Could they by any chance have been Mr. Bobbsey and the trappers, Sakey and Joslind?

Nogasak had given the men wrong instructions as to the direction to take. The cruel Eskimo had said that he thought the white men would never find White Hope. He had misdirected them purposely, in belief that they would lose themselves in that dreary white waste and die of exposure or hunger, possibly both. Bert couldn't understand how anyone could be as mean as Nogasak. It frightened him to think of what might happen to his father, and he felt that he ought to start out at once to find him and warn him of the danger that lay before him.

On the way back to the settlement Bert was trying to figure out how he could tell his mother what Nogasak had said. He knew that he must let her know about it. She would be very angry if she should find out later that he had kept anything as important as this from her. Bert knew that the only thing for him to do would be to tell her; yet to do so would be very hard.

However, Mrs. Bobbsey took the news much more calmly than Bert had thought she would. For a moment she drew her son close to her and pressed her hand over her eyes. When she took it away her face was composed again.

"We must not think the worst, Bert. Your father would want us to be cheerful. We must believe that he has reached White Hope safely and will be with us again soon. We *will* believe it," she added courageously. "I feel that he will come back to us."

Mrs. Bobbsey could not know as she spoke how

soon her faith would be tested to the utmost. That night was the night of the heavy snow. It began about nightfall. There was a sudden wild gale, and the wind whistled about, shaking buildings and piling white flakes against doors and windows.

Men returned to the settlement, puffing and blowing, half-frozen by the bitter wind. Doctor Bramley came into the big main room looking like Santa Claus himself. The children laughed as he shook himself, and the snow flew from him in every direction.

"Anuk says the snow is several feet deep already," reported the good doctor. "Our dogs had all they could do to get back here. I pity any poor fellows caught out in this storm tonight.

"By the way," he added, taking off his mittens and rubbing his hands to warm them, "I understand from Anuk that Nogasak disappeared early this afternoon, taking his dogs with him. Small loss," the man went on, staring into the fire and thoughtfully stirring with his boot a piece of charred wood that had fallen on the hearth. "The fellow was a trouble-maker if I ever saw one. I'm glad he is gone."

Bert saw his mother's glance turn to the window where the snow had already drifted thickly against the pane. He knew that she was thinking of Daddy Bobbsey, and wondering where he was and whether he had reached White Hope safely. Bert felt very anxious, too, but he decided to be as cheerful as he could for his mother's sake. He would have to be the man of the family until his father's return.

All that night the wind howled about the settlement buildings, driving the snow before it in blinding sheets, and piling it high about doors and windows.

When the small twins opened their eyes the next morning they found their room filled with a dim twilight. The snow had drifted so high about the windows that almost all the outdoor light was shut out. They were imprisoned in a tight little indoor world, bounded by four walls.

Flossie and Freddie were thrilled by the new experience. They had never seen such a snowstorm before. They traced designs on the frosted window-panes. Freddie even climbed on a chair to see if he could look over the big white drift that reached almost to the top of his window.

"I've never seen such a big snow," he cried. "Golly, I guess it must be about nine feet deep."

"I bet it's a hundred," said Flossie. "Maybe it reaches right up to the top of this building."

"I bet it doesn't," said Freddie. "It doesn't reach half-way up to the roof."

"Anyway, I wish Daddy would come," sighed Flossie. "He's been away an awful long time."

Now Puk came along the passage, soft-footed in his leather moccasins. His round face broke into a happy grin when he saw the children.

"Breakfast ready," he cried. "You come."

While at their morning meal Miss Lamson said that she was worried about the food supply at the settlement. The heavy storm, coming unexpectedly and much earlier than it had in previous years, had caught them at a time when they had very little on hand to eat.

"We expect a large consignment of canned goods, cured meats and dried fruits by the next Bay steamer," the teacher explained. "But if the snow continues it will be almost impossible to get a dog team through to the dock. Then there is the chance, too," she added, "that the steamer may be held up by ice in the river."

"Dear me," sighed Mrs. Bobbsey. "I do hope nothing will happen to the boats. Certainly we cannot spend the winter here."

"I know you wish to take the last ship bound south," agreed the teacher seriously.

"Are we dangerously short of supplies now?" asked the twins' mother.

"If we can tunnel through to the stone hut where the foodstuffs are kept we shall have enough to last us for several days. But the place is probably buried to the roof by the snow. My people are so busy digging paths to the dog-shed and other settlement buildings that I can't spare any of them just now for the work of tunnelling to the supply hut."

"Why, I can do that," Bert said eagerly. "Back in Lakeport I often make tunnels in the snow just for the fun of it. Puk will help me. Won't you, Puk?"

"And so will I," said Freddy manfully.

"Do you think you could?" asked Miss Lamson doubtfully. "It's very hard work, you know."

"We are not afraid of hard work," said Bert. "It'll be fun. When do we start, and where are the shovels?"

"Out in the woodshed," said the teacher. "I don't know how to thank you boys," she added gratefully. "You have taken a big worry off my mind."

As soon as breakfast was over the lads set to work. Nan and Flossie would have been glad to have helped too, but Miss Lamson had no more tools to give them.

Puk and Bert worked manfully, and little Freddie did his very best to help. Throughout the hours of the morning they shovelled snow, digging deeper and deeper through the heavy drifts that separated the main house from the supply hut. Although their muscles ached and their backs felt almost broken, they kept at the work.

At last their efforts won out. Bert's shovel scraped against something hard and firm. He brushed the top of it clear of snow, and found beneath his hand a cold, smooth surface of rock.

"We're at the hut, all right," he called to Puk. "Do you know where the door is? We don't want to waste time digging in the wrong place."

"Door right here some place," said Puk. "We find him pretty soon."

Ten minutes more of heavy work and they located the door. What a relief it was to find it! The boys pushed it open and stepped inside the hut.

They filled their arms with foodstuffs. Bert took some canned goods. Puk slung a huge cured ham over his shoulder. Freddie found a jar of pineapple and a bag of flour, which he carried as his share of the load.

Miss Lamson was delighted with their success.

"The food in the hut will not last us more than three or four days," said the teacher. "If the snow has stopped by that time, then we will have to find some way to get a dog team through to the steamer dock."

"We'll help to get the food any time that the team can get through," offered Bert Bobbsey.

"Well, we'll see when the weather breaks," answered Miss Lamson.

The third day dawned clear, with the sun coming out a little. Their supplies were so low now that it was decided to send two dogsleds through to the depot, in the hope that they would return safely with the necessary foodstuffs.

"Is Anuk going to drive, Puk?" asked the older Bobbsey boy of his friend.

"Think yes," answered the Eskimo lad.

"Hurray!" shouted Bert. "I'm going to beg to be taken along!"

CHAPTER XV

DEEP SNOW

AFTER much coaxing the boys succeeded in getting permission to go. Anuk proved to be an unexpected friend. He was short-handed, he said, and would appreciate the boys' help in loading the sleds. Their aid on the return trip would also be very necessary, he stated.

"Let them come. They very good boys and work hard," said Anuk.

As it happened, the task of getting the sleds to and from the depot was far more difficult than Bert had thought it would be. All trails had been wiped out by the heavy snowfall. The drifts were deep. Often the huskies would be floundering through snow that reached over their shoulders. Several times, despite Anuk's efforts to keep to the ridges and higher ground, the dogs sank over their heads in the clinging snow and had to be pulled out.

Once the sled overturned, flinging the boys out, head over heels. They picked themselves up, however, helped to right the sled, and struggled on.

Finally, after many hours of such effort, they reached the steamer dock. The sleds were loaded hurriedly, for Anuk wanted to get back to the settlement before dark.

"More snow come, maybe," he grunted with an anxious glance at the sky. "We hurry."

The return journey was much easier. The temperature had fallen many degrees, and the intense cold had hardened the snow, forming over it a thin crust of ice. This was thick enough to bear the weight of the huskies, and in some places even the sleds. The tracks they had made on the outward trip were still there and served to blaze a kind of trail for them.

The early dusk had fallen by the time they reached the settlement. Everyone turned out to greet them. A dozen hands were immediately at their service to help carry the supplies to the stone hut and the house.

Flossie, curious as always, took a large, knobby package from the pile of foodstuffs. "My, I wonder what this is," she said, poking at it with a chubby finger. "It feels like a lot of walnuts."

The little girl probably gave the bag one poke too many. At any rate the wrapping broke, and out popped dozens of pieces of dried fruit.

As luck would have it, Flossie dropped the fruit at the feet of the ravenous dogs. Before a person could have said Christopher Columbus every single one of the shrivelled little balls had disappeared, having been gobbled up by the huskies.

"Oh, I'm sorry," cried Flossie in dismay. "I didn't mean to drop the fruit."

"Flossie, Flossie, will you ever learn to let things alone when they don't belong to you?" chided Mrs. Bobbsey. "You must not touch anything else," she added, as Flossie reached eagerly to help with the unloading.

The little girl felt she was in disgrace. She stood aside while the others passed back and forth, busily unloading the sleds. She wished she had not been so careless with the package of dried fruit. It would have been such fun to have helped unpack everything.

Freddie paused on his way to the house to console his twin. "I wouldn't worry too much about the fruit," he whispered. "I think it won't make the dogs sick. There's a lot more in another package, too. Bert said there was."

That night Miss Lamson celebrated the safe arrival of the sleds by ordering that a big meal be prepared and served to everyone in the settlement. And how good everything tasted There were slices of broiled ham swimming in cream gravy, small potatoes, carrots and peas—canned, but good just the same—and boiled onions. For dessert they had plum pudding with hard sauce.

Nan scraped the last of the dessert from her plate and leaned back in her chair.

However, Puk and Nyla, as guests of the Bobbsey children, ate very little. "Funny food," they grunted. "Too much." Indeed, the Eskimo children were not used to so many different kinds of food to eat, as fish and meat were about the only things they ever ate.

"I've never had a nicer dinner, except at Thanksgiving and Christmas," Nan explained. "If only Daddy were here," she added with a sober glance about the table, "everything would be perfect."

"I hope Daddy comes soon," said Flossie wistfully. "I can't wait!"

"Golly! He has been away an awful long time," agreed Freddie "Isn't he coming home pretty soon, Mother?"

"I hope so, dear," said Mrs. Bobbsey earnestly. "I hope and pray that he will come back to us soon—or that we will get some good word from him."

"We are sure to have news of him soon," said Miss Lamson comfortingly. "Who knows but that we may hear from him tomorrow?"

However, no clue of Mr. Bobbsey reached the settlement the next day or the one after that. The third day, however, brought a stranger to the camp with the news that three white men had been discovered in a place several days' journey from White Hope. With their native runners and a half-starved team of huskies, they had been overtaken by the blizzard and forced to seek shelter in a deserted hut. The men were safe, the stranger said, but their supplies were running low. It would be necessary to get food to them at once if they were not to die from cold and hunger.

"Can you tell me about my daddy?" asked Freddie.

From the description the stranger gave of the three white men, Mrs. Bobbsey and the twins felt sure that they must be Mr. Bobbsey and the trappers, Sakey and Joslind.

"I wish I could telephone to my dear daddy," said Flossie.

Of course, the news caused a great deal of excitement at the settlement. The twins wanted to set off at once with food to their father. Mrs. Bobbsey did not think this would be a good idea, so it was finally decided that Anuk should undertake the trip.

A sled was brought out at once and Bert helped to pack it with all necessary supplies. When the dogs were harnessed and the Eskimo appeared with his dog-lash, Bert begged to be taken along.

Anuk agreed to take Puk and Bert with him for a short distance. He told the lads to wear their heaviest boots and to arm themselves with the long spears, chief weapon of the Eskimos.

"You walk back alone," grunted Anuk. "You need spear maybe. You take."

So, thus armed and dressed in their heaviest furs, the two lads started off with Anuk. The day was clear and very cold. The snow was now covered with a thick coating of ice. Anuk cracked his whip in the frosty air. The huskies, led by the handsome lead dog Palla, fairly flew over the shining ice.

"We make good time," Anuk said to Bert. "We find your father very soon."

"I hope so," replied the lad. After a moment he added, "I wish I could go all the way with you, Anuk."

"Your mother no like," grunted Anuk. "We go little way. Then you get out. Walk back."

Bert said no more. He knew it would be useless to argue with Anuk.

Their way led them over several small bodies of water, frozen now until they were as solid as the land itself.

"Anuk go short way now, over water," Puk

explained. "In the spring ice break up. Then Anuk go long way, around water."

All too soon for Bert and Puk, the driver pulled the dogs to a standstill. "Come far enough," he grunted. "You go back now."

"Give my love to Dad when you see him," said Bert. "Tell him to come back to us as soon as he can."

Anuk nodded, and cracked the lash over the backs of the huskies. "Me tell him," he promised.

The boys watched until the Eskimo and the flying team were out of sight. Then they turned back to the settlement, wishing they might have gone along.

Puk led the way. Bert wondered how he knew just where to go when the whole landscape, as far as the white boy could see, was just one great, unbroken stretch of gleaming snow and ice. Puk did not hesitate, nor did he stop to look about him except when a flock of big birds flapped heavily overhead. He led the way back to the settlement as straight as a crow could fly.

Suddenly he paused. With his spear he pointed to a dark object that stood out against the gleaming sea of ice. Puk's eyes gleamed.

"Him seal," said Puk. "We kill him. Take him back with us. Much good to eat."

CHAPTER XVI

THE WALRUS

BERT had never seen a live seal in its native habitat, much less attempted to kill one. He admired the Eskimo lad greatly because he was not afraid to tackle the big sea beast.

Swiftly the two boys sped over the snow. Puk took the lead, his spear held ready for the kill. Only once Puk paused to say to Bert:

"Him walrus. Big one!"

The huge black-looking mass did not move until the lads had almost reached it. Then it let out a deep roar, and lumbered across the ice directly towards Bert! The lad hastily leaped to one side, forgetting to use his spear, although Puk called to him to do so.

Now the walrus slithered about on the ice and made towards Puk. The Eskimo lad did not jump aside as Bert had done, but stood still and waited, his spear poised.

When the animal was within a few feet of him, he threw the weapon. It gleamed in the air for just a second before he hurled it into the body of the walrus.

"That get him!" cried Puk. "One thrust of spear, walrus die. Now we get him back to settlement. Miss

Lamson like, everybody like. We have much good feast."

However, the task of pulling the dead walrus over the ice to the settlement was not an easy one. Puk was strong from a life spent in the healthful North country. Bert was very husky for his age, too. Yet both of them were only boys, and the walrus was a huge beast. Bert looked at the big bulk.

"We fix," said Puk.

The lad drew aside his parka, disclosing a coil of rope which he had slung over his shoulders before he had left the settlement. Puk unwound it, and with Bert's help passed it about the body of the walrus and fastened it tightly.

"We both pull," said Puk, taking hold of the rope and motioning to Bert to do likewise. "Pretty soon you push, I pull. We fix him fine."

In spite of Puk's confidence, the lads found it a long, hard trip back to the settlement. Downward slopes were not so difficult, but on the upgrades the boys had to pull and tug until their muscles were sore and their lungs ached when they tried to breathe.

Finally they came in sight of their destination. Both boys sat down on the stiff carcass of the walrus to rest and breathe deeply.

"Do you think we can make it?" asked Bert.

"Sure," said Puk. "We make."

The last pull was the hardest of all. The boys succeeded, however, and came into camp dragging the big walrus behind them.

Great was the rejoicing at the settlement when the lads brought in Puk's kill. Fresh meat was very scarce during the winter season. Juicy walrus steaks cooked over a fire in the open would be a treat to whites and natives alike.

Miss Lamson decided to celebrate it, and invited Eskimos from neighbouring villages to take part in a great outdoor feast. Runners were sent out to spread the good news, while others at the settlement were kept busy preparing the meat for roasting.

"A party . . . a party," cried little Nyla, clapping her hands.

Nan, Freddie, and Flossie were very proud of Bert. They looked upon him as a mighty hunter.

"But I didn't kill the walrus. It was Puk who did it," explained the older Bobbsey boy.

However, no one would believe that Puk had done it all, even when Bert told them over and over that this was so. And so the lad found himself raised to the position of a hero, though this was done much against his wishes.

Preparations for the big feast went forward rapidly. By dusk a fire was roaring in the open space in front of the settlement. The appetizing odour of sizzling fresh meat filled the air, and the Eskimos, men, women, and children, began coming in from neighbouring villages.

"Doesn't it smell grand here?" cried Freddie. "I wish Dinah could be here. I bet she'd like this smell."

The newcomers gathered about the fire with the people from the settlement. To each of them was given a bowl of steaming broth thick with rice, and rich with the fat they liked so well. Afterwards came the juicy walrus meat, which they ate with as much relish as if they were starved.

"Isn't this the best fun," laughed Nan. "A picnic in the snow."

When the feast was over, two of the Eskimos moved into the circle of firelight and began to dance. The others shouted and clapped in time to the whirling and stamping.

Flossie, who could never keep her feet still when others were dancing, was unable to be quiet. She jumped up, pulled her little brother Freddie by the hand, and drew him into the circle of firelight. Before the little boy knew just what it was all about, he found himself going through some fancy steps he had learned with Flossie, and had given one time at a school entertainment.

Gradually the native dancers gave place to the little white children, although the hand-clapping and the queer, droning music kept right on. When the Bobbseys finished, Flossie curtsied and Freddie bowed as they had been taught to do. Their audience shouted gleefully.

"More," they cried. "More dance!"

But Freddie suddenly grew bashful and refused to do a thing. Flossie curtsied again and backed away. Suddenly she stumbled over an uneven place in the ground and nearly fell into the fire! Nan caught her little sister by the hand and pulled her away from the danger.

As the older girl did so, the light from the fire gleamed on her wrist-watch. One of the Eskimos bent towards her and pointed to it.

"That—tell time?" he asked.

Nan replied that it did, and the Eskimo immediately asked another question.

"How—tell time? You teach—please."

To oblige him, Nan removed her watch and leaned closer to the light thrown by the fire.

"I'll show you," she said. "Now, you see the figures on the face of the watch are all numbers which you have learned from Miss Lamson and the other teachers. They go from one to twelve. You count with me—one, two, three—that's right. All the way up to twelve."

Other natives gathered round, listening to Nan. They really made a great effort to understand what she was saying, and they went over, again and again, what she told them, repeating her words as they did so. Some of them seemed to grasp her meaning; others grew more and more puzzled the longer she went on; still others became tired very quickly and wandered off to join in another form of entertainment.

No one could say just what time the party began to break up. The Eskimos just seemed to fade away from the circle and slip out into the darkness. They went as silently as a company of ghosts, until finally only the people of the settlement were left. These drifted away after a little while. Miss Lamson lingered behind to make sure that the fire was properly put out.

"My, that was fun," said Flossie later, as Nan helped her to undress. "I wish we could have another party tomorrow. But I don't suppose we could very well ask Bert and Puk to kill another walrus so soon."

"I'm afraid he might think we were a little bit unreasonable," laughed Nan. She tucked her small sister into bed and gave her a good night kiss. "Sleep well, dear, and sweet dreams."

"Good night," said Flossie sleepily.

The next morning Nan made a startling discovery. Her wrist-watch had disappeared!

"I must have lost it last night when I was teaching the Eskimos how to tell time," she said. "I thought I put it right back on my arm, but I guess I didn't. Oh, dear!"

"Now, don't worry," Mrs. Bobbsey soothed her daughter. "If you dropped it near the fire you will surely find it. The children will help you search for it."

"Of course we will," said Freddie. "Come on, we'll look all over."

However, they could not find the watch, although they searched the scene of the former night's party very thoroughly. Their hunt included all the buildings of the settlement. Several of Miss Lamson's people were questioned, but not one could be found who knew anything about the lost watch.

Finally Freddie asked Nan if she would go with him to the village where Looktoo, the medicine-man, lived with his people.

"Looktoo is a very wise man," Freddie pointed out. "He knew about Mr. Weller being at White Hope, you know. Maybe he can tell you where your watch is, too."

More to humour Freddie than because she believed in what he said, Nan went with him to the Eskimo village. When they arrived there the little boy led her straight to Looktoo's igloo.

As they entered the hut, after the old man had told them to come in, they found Looktoo sitting cross-legged on his bearskin rug. In his wrinkled fingers was Nan's wrist-watch!

CHAPTER XVII

LOOKTOO

NAN gave a cry of surprise and delight.

"Oh, so it was *you* who found it!" she said, moving towards the old man. "You have found my wristwatch. Oh, please give it to me. I am so glad to see it again."

She held out her hand for the timepiece, but Looktoo scowled and drew back.

"Watch belong Looktoo," he said. "You no can take."

"But Looktoo, you'd better give Nan her watch," said Freddie hotly. "It belongs to her. She lost it last night. You can't very well keep a thing that belongs to someone else, can you? It's—it's like *stealing*!"

"Sh, Freddie," warned Nan. "I think I can manage this all right."

Carefully the girl explained how she had lost the watch; how she and her brothers and sister had looked for it all morning, and how she and Freddie had decided to come to Looktoo's hut to ask about it.

"You will give it back to me, won't you?" she pleaded.

But the medicine-man was stubborn. The watch

was a charm, he said, and would keep away evil spirits. It would help him to become more powerful over the people of his village.

"Sick Eskimo find—give it to Looktoo. Looktoo keep."

"Why did the sick Eskimo give it to you?" asked Nan.

"Looktoo make sick Eskimo well. Sick Eskimo give Looktoo watch."

After much persuasion Nan finally got the medicine-man to take her and Freddie to see his patient. Grumbling, he led the way to another hut. On some furs in one corner of the place lay a sick man; Nan could tell at a glance that he was very ill indeed. His eyes were bright with fever, and he tossed about constantly on his couch of furs.

The girl went over and put her hand on the Eskimo's forehead. It was, as she thought it would be, very hot. Looktoo bent over the sick man and put a question to him, pointing to Nan's watch.

A look of understanding came into the eyes of the Eskimo. He nodded once in reply to a question. Then his eyes grew glassy again and he began to toss and mutter strange things.

"He say, give charm to Looktoo," said the medicine-man. "Looktoo keep."

"We'll see about that," said Nan under her breath.

She felt that it was useless to argue with the "doctor" any longer. Taking Freddie by the hand, she started to go back to the settlement.

"I think Looktoo's mean," said the little boy, his short legs trying hard to keep up with his sister's longer ones. "I never thought he would keep your watch, Nan."

"I think we will get it back, Freddie," said Nan, half-running in her eagerness to reach the settlement. "I have a plan, and I hope it works out the way I want it to. Can't you walk any faster, Freddie?"

"Well," said the little fellow, "I'm pretty nearly running now, you know. But I'll do my best."

When they arrived Nan found everybody very much interested in her story and very eager to help her get back her watch. Nyla, Bert and Puk offered to go with her to the village to try to change the mind of the stubborn old Eskimo.

Mrs. Bobbsey also offered to go with them. Her heart had been touched by Nan's story of the sick man. She wanted to see for herself just how ill he was, with the thought that if he were in need of attention she would ask Doctor Bramley to have him brought to the little hospital at the settlement where he would be given proper care.

They all set out for Looktoo's village, Mrs. Bobbsey carrying her first-aid kit of ready medicines which she had brought with her from Lakeport. The medicine-man's anger increased when he saw the group from the settlement. At first he refused to listen to argument; it was not until Mrs. Bobbsey showed him a handful of coins in "white man's money" that he changed his mind.

"We will give you all these if you will return to me my daughter's watch," Mrs. Bobbsey said. "These pieces of money will probably do you more good than a watch, anyway. You can buy many trinkets with them and presents for your people when the steamer comes in."

Looktoo finally was won over, though he did so very grudgingly. He had counted a good deal upon the power Nan's charm would have given him over the people of his village.

When Mrs. Bobbsey said she would like to see the sick Eskimo, Looktoo took her to the hut where the man lay. The patient's fever was higher. He rolled and tossed, muttering to himself all the while. As soon as she saw him, Mrs. Bobbsey knew that this was a case for Doctor Bramley to handle. She was sure that if the man was not given aid very soon, he would die.

Mrs. Bobbsey did what she could for the sick native. She gave him some fever pills from the first-aid kit. She bathed his face with cold water, and straightened the rumpled furs under him.

"Poor fellow," she said. "He needs to lie between cool sheets with only a light blanket to cover him. These furs are making his condition worse, and I am sure the medicine he is getting is not doing him any good."

"Shouldn't we take him to the settlement, Mother?" asked Nan.

"As soon as possible, if we are to save his life," agreed Mrs. Bobbsey. "I shall get in touch with Dr. Bramley at once."

Looktoo watched them leave the village, a suspicious gleam in his eye. The more he thought of the strange white woman coming into his hut the greater grew his dislike for the settlement workers. She had robbed him of his "charm", he thought, which would have given him great influence with his people. Now she threatened to take from him his patient as well.

Looktoo was the one to cure the sick of his village, he felt. He did not need the aid of the white doctor. Suddenly the Eskimo decided that he hated all white people. He raised his fist and shook it in the direction of the settlement.

"Me fix you," he grunted.

The sick Eskimo was removed to the little hospital where he was placed between clean sheets. The right kind of medicine was given him by Dr. Bramley, and he was coaxed by Nan, with Flossie helping her to take something to eat.

"I can carry tea and never spill it," said Flossie to Bert.

The twins proved themselves to be of great help to the nurse at this time. Scarcely a day passed by that new cases did not come to the settlement—a number of these were from Looktoo's own village—so that the red-haired nurse was very grateful to the Bobbsey children for assisting her. She said that she would not have known how to do all her work without them.

"I've learned a lot of Eskimo words," said Bert proudly.

The twins took almost entire charge of the sick native they had brought from Looktoo's village.

"We are really responsible for his being here," Nan pointed out. "So of course it is up to us to see that he gets well."

"I can make sure that he gets his medicine on time," said Flossie.

"Maybe I can give him an alcohol rub," said Freddie. "I saw Nurse do it once. I'm sure I know how."

Under the care of the Bobbsey twins the patient began to get much better. His temperature dropped, and he was able, as time went on, to take more nourishment. One day he even went so far as to smile at his young nurses. The twins were delighted, and at once tried harder than ever to do things for him.

"I never knew it was so much fun to make sick people well," said Flossie. "I think I'll be a nurse when I grow up."

Meanwhile, under Miss Lamson's direction Freddie and Bert set up a large United States flag in front of the settlement. It had been made by hand by the people there, who had worked a long time trying to make it as perfect as possible. It was a token to Miss Lamson and her country. Great was the rejoicing, therefore, when it was raised for the first time, its stars and stripes waving bravely in the wind.

"It's a great old flag!" said Bert, staring up at it.

Freddie borrowed Nyla's music-box for the affair. Its tunes played merrily in the frosty air while the children joined in singing.

"I guess it's the best in the world," said Freddie. "Anyway, I think so."

A day or so after the raising of the stars and stripes Freddie and Flossie were romping near one of the settlement buildings when they saw an old bent

Eskimo creep out of the shadows and stand there for a moment, staring upwards.

"It's Looktoo," Freddie whispered. "I wonder what he wants here?"

Suddenly the Eskimo lifted an old gun he was carrying, fitted it to his shoulder, and fired deliberately at the United States flag!

CHAPTER XVIII

A WILD RIDE

LOOKTOO had shot at the United States flag!

For a moment Freddie and Flossie were so astonished and so angry that they could not move. While the children stood there looking towards him, the man raised his ancient weapon and fired again. This time the bullet tore straight through the waving stars and stripes!

"Say, you stop that!" cried Freddie, running forward.

At the same moment several doors at the settlement were opened and people hurried out. Bert and Puk were the first to reach the flag-pole but by the time they got there, Looktoo, with a quickness surprising in such an old man, had disappeared.

"Who fired those shots?" cried Bert.

"It was Looktoo, the medicine-man," cried Freddie, jumping up and down in excitement. "He shot at our flag."

"And then he ran away," added Flossie.

Bert and Puk hurried over to the two small twins.

"Which way did he go?" Bert demanded. "Did you notice?"

"Over there," said Freddie, pointing.

133

"Behind that building," Flossie added.

Bert and Puk darted after Looktoo. In and out among the various structures they went, searching in every corner. At first it seemed that the medicine-man must have escaped for sure, though how he could have got out of sight without going into one of the buildings the boys could not understand.

"How could he disappear like that, all of a sudden?" demanded Bert. "I don't see how he'd dare to go into any place around here."

Puk was about to reply, when a sharp baying from the dog sheds startled both lads. A look passed between them, and they darted towards the place where the sounds came from.

"That Poto make noise," said Puk, as Bert wrenched open the door.

The boys were just in time to seize Looktoo and pull his gun away from him. The Eskimo was backed against the wall of the shed, all the while hold-ing the weapon above his head ready to strike. In another moment he would have crashed the heavy stock of the gun down upon the skull of the nearest husky.

Both Puk and Bert were furious with him, Bert because of the insult he had offered to the flag, Puk because he was going to kill Poto. The two lads dragged Looktoo out of the shed. There they were met by some people from the settlement who had been attracted to the place by the dog's baying.

"Looktoo shot at the flag!" cried Bert indignantly. "The twins saw him."

"He shot at it twice!" added Flossie.

There was an angry movement among the group. Miss Lamson stepped forward to speak to Looktoo.

"Why did you do it?" she demanded sternly. "Why did you shoot at our flag?"

The Eskimo scowled. He raised his fist and shook it angrily.

"Your people flag—no good," he growled. "White people—no good."

Again there were angry mutterings among those gathered there, but with a gesture of her hand Miss Lamson held them back.

"Let the man speak" she demanded. Then turning to Looktoo, she said sternly, "Go on!"

"Looktoo good medicine-man," returned the Eskimo. "Looktoo cure sick Eskimo. People of village say Looktoo good medicine-man."

"Go on!" prompted Miss Lamson patiently.

"Then white people, they come. They say Looktoo no good, no cure sick Eskimo. Pretty soon people of village say, 'Looktoo no good, no cure sick Eskimo.' They go get white medicine-man."

"A case of jealousy, I guess," said Doctor Bramley from the background.

Miss Lamson gave him a quick glance, then continued to question Looktoo.

"So, because some of your sick people have come to the settlement for treatment since they have more faith in our white medicine-man than they have in Looktoo, you are angry with all white people. Is that it?"

"White man—no good," growled Looktoo.

"So you come down here and shoot at the white

man's flag," said Miss Lamson, still stern. "That is very bad, Looktoo. The white man loves his flag. He will let no one insult it. Do you know what you must do for shooting at our flag?"

Looktoo shifted his feet uneasily, but made no answer.

"You must kiss the flag," ordered Miss Lamson.

Quickly the Bobbsey children helped to lower the ensign. When he saw the looks on the faces of those about him, the Eskimo grudgingly put his face against the stars and stripes. Then Bert raised the emblem again.

Looktoo shuffled his feet still more, and shot an angry glance at Miss Lamson.

"Now you must never shoot at our flag again. You must keep away from the settlement altogether, Looktoo. If you ever come back this way something very bad will happen to you. Do you understand?"

Looktoo nodded. He took an uneasy step backwards, his eyes on the tall flag-pole.

"Me go now," he grunted. "No come again—never."

"Good," said Miss Lamson. "See that you keep your word!"

The twins thought that Looktoo had been let off much too easily. Miss Lamson, however, did not agree with them. She pointed out that the medicine-man had been badly frightened and would most likely be very careful to stay away from the place in the future.

"He is losing out in his own village, too," she added. "His people will drive him away before long and he will have to find a home with some other tribe. I think," she added, "that we will have no more trouble with Looktoo."

The following day Anuk returned. The Eskimo was at the point of exhaustion, and he brought only bad news.

"Snow very deep," he said when Mrs. Bobbsey and Miss Lamson eagerly questioned him. "All trails gone. Mr. Bobbsey, Joslind, Sakey, Anuk no find. Anuk look one day, two, three, more maybe. No see trappers, white man."

"Oh, but what shall we do!" cried Mrs. Bobbsey desperately. "Somebody must find Richard. Someone must help him, if I have to go out and look for him myself! Oh, this is terrible, terrible!"

While Nan tried to comfort her mother, Miss Lamson promised that another search would be started for Mr. Bobbsey as soon as possible. Meanwhile Freddie and Flossie were having an adventure of their own. It was the little boy who had discovered Anuk's sled. The dogs were still in harness. The whole outfit had been left unguarded for the time being while the Eskimo made his report to Miss Lamson and Mrs. Bobbsey.

Freddie jumped on to the sled as he had so often seen Anuk do. He seized the reins and waved the whip over his head.

"Get in, Flossie," he invited. "I'll take you for a ride."

For a moment the little girl hesitated. "Do you think Mother would want us to?" she asked.

"Sure, she won't mind," said Freddie, though in

his heart he was by no means certain of this. "Anyway, we won't go very far. Hurry up, get in before somebody comes."

Flossie jumped into the sled and held on for dear life while Freddie waved the whip and called to the dogs. The huskies, tired as they were, obeyed the tug of the reins and the crack of the whip.

Palla, the lead dog, put his weight against the harness, the others did the same, and off they sped at a good clip over the frosty ground. The twins saw Anuk run out of the house and heard him shout something to them.

Freddie could not have stopped the dogs now if he had wanted to. Perhaps he had cracked the whip a little too hard, or maybe he had flicked one or two of the huskies with it without meaning to do so. At any rate, the dogs had started to bolt, and paid no attention whatsoever to Freddie or to his shouts to them to stop.

Out on to a ridge of ice raced the dogs, led by Palla. The huskies strained against the harness, while the runners made a singing noise as the sled flew along behind them. Suddenly Freddie gave a cry of alarm and pulled with all his might at the reins. Just before them the ridge ended. The ground dropped away abruptly to a lower level some dozen feet below!

Freddie and Flossie were badly frightened.

"Stop! Stop!" cried Flossie. "Don't let the dogs run away, Freddie!"

"Whoa! Whoa!" shouted the small boy, but the animals raced on madly. "I—I *can't* st—st—stop them!" gasped the Bobbsey boy in alarm.

CHAPTER XIX

THE LEAD DOG

IT seemed for a moment as if nothing could prevent the small twins from plunging, sled and all, over the edge of the ridge. It was Palla who saved them. The lead dog stopped suddenly, its four paws rigidly braced against the weight of the sled.

The other animals flung themselves backwards. Their nails made a rasping sound as they slid over the icy ground. The weight of the sled pushed them forward closer and closer to the sharp drop.

Suddenly Palla disappeared.

It took Flossie and Freddie a moment or two to realize that the sled had come to a full stop. But the beautiful dog was gone! The children quickly stepped out on to the slippery ridge, and ran to help Palla.

Then Anuk rushed up with some other men from the settlement.

"You try kill my huskies?" cried the man in a rage. "Palla—where is he?"

"I'm afraid he fell over the edge," said Freddie sadly.

"He was trying to hold the sled back, but it kept pushing him," Flossie added.

139

Anuk wasted no more time in words, but rushed to Palla's help. The twins followed, feeling very guilty and very much ashamed of themselves.

They found Palla dangling in the harness over the edge of the drop. The other huskies had kept him from falling any farther. They had crouched to bear the weight of the lead dog, their bodies braced, their sharp nails digging into the ice.

With Anuk's help Palla was able to scramble up on to the ice. With the aid of other men from the settlement the sled was drawn backwards along the dangerous ridge until the ground widened enough to be able to turn the sled and head it once more towards home.

Palla was hurt. His feet were torn and bleeding; one shoulder was badly gashed by a sharp splinter of ice.

Anuk was very angry with the twins. He scolded them loudly while he unharnessed his beautiful dog.

"You walk back. Palla ride in sled. Palla good dog. You very bad white children."

Freddie and Flossie took Anuk's scolding meekly. They knew they had done wrong in taking the sled without permission, and they were very sorry that Palla had been hurt. Besides this, they had been rather badly frightened by their adventure; in fact, enough so to cause them to try to be good for a long time to come.

When they arrived at the settlement the twins begged to be allowed to nurse Palla. Anuk gave them permission after some argument, for he was still very angry with the white children.

Flossie brought some salve and a roll of white bandage from the house, while Freddie followed, staggering under the weight of a bucket of warm water.

Then, under Anuk's instructions, Flossie bathed and bandaged the dog's wounds, her chubby little hands working very gently. Palla made no protest, although the treatment must have hurt him a good deal. He seemed to know, wise dog that he was, that everything was being done for his good.

"There, I think he will be all right now," said Flossie, as she looked at the result of her work with satisfaction. "We will be over later to see how he is getting along."

"We might bring him some pills," said Freddie.

Meanwhile, the failure of Anuk's mission in regard to Mr. Bobbsey and the trappers, Sakey and Joslind, had made everyone in the settlement feel very sad. It was agreed that, even though Anuk had been unable to find the white men, no one would have been able to have done so.

Miss Lamson tried very hard to cheer Mrs. Bobbsey by pointing out that Mr. Bobbsey, Sakey and Joslind might have shot or speared some game, so that they would have something to eat and not starve to death. "In which case they may have gone on to White Hope, and are there safe and sound by now. At any time we may hear good news of them," she told her friend.

Meanwhile, life at the settlement went on much the same as usual. Under the good care given him by Freddie and Flossie, Palla grew well and strong again, and Anuk began to forget his hard feelings towards the white children.

The friendship between Nan and Nyla, and Bert and Puk grew stronger every day. Nyla thought Nan was very pretty. She had formed the habit of watching the white girl as she combed her hair before the cracked mirror in the girls' bedroom. Nan would often see the little Eskimo girl's round eyes and solemn face wistfully regarding her in the looking-glass. One day Nan said to her:

"How would you like me to curl your hair, Nyla, and dress you in one of my frocks? I could borrow Mother's curling-iron."

Nyla's face lighted up, and she smiled broadly. "Nyla like. Curl hair, please!" she said.

So Nan set to work. She placed her friend in front of the mirror, while Flossie ran for Mother Bobbsey's curling-iron. While it was being heated Nan combed out Nyla's short, straight locks.

"You have nice hair, Nyla, very strong and thick. It should take a pretty curl. Now, how would you like it arranged, away from your face or towards your face with a parting, or just brushed straight back? I can fix it any way you like."

Nyla did not know what to say. She only looked puzzled and shook her head at Nan's questions.

"Any way *you* like," she said. "You fix."

"I think you better curl it around her face," Flossie suggested. "It will make her look prettier."

Nyla's white teeth flashed. "Nyla no pretty," she said shyly.

"You just wait and see," Nan told her.

For a short while all three girls were busy watching Nyla's reflection in the mirror. Flossie knelt on a chair so that she would get a better view. The Eskimo girl's round face with its high cheek-bones looked very serious as Nan's busy fingers handled the curling-iron.

"You *have* nice hair," said Nan, patting the waves into place, "the kind that stays put. Now mine," she added, with a glance at her own pretty head, "flies all over when I brush it hard."

"Your hair very pretty," said the Eskimo girl with a smile. "Nyla like very much."

"Yours is going to be pretty, too, when Nan gets through with it," said Flossie. "Don't you like it, Nyla?"

The native girl nodded, her face a broad smile. "No look like Nyla any more. Look like white girl," she said.

When she saw her own reflection in the mirror, it made her feel funny. Her round eyes got bigger and bigger. She could scarcely draw her gaze away even when Nan said gaily:

"I am going to have you put on one of my wool dresses, Nyla, the light-blue one. Wait until you see yourself in it! You just won't know who you are!"

The Eskimo stood very still as Nan slipped the blue dress over her head and buttoned it up at the throat. Then she fastened the belt and smoothed the cloth evenly over the girl's chunky shoulders.

"Now," Nan said, "look at yourself!"

Nyla stole a shy glance at her reflection, then broke into giggles and clapped her hands over her face. She refused to look again, until Nan said she would have to take away the blue dress if the little Eskimo kept on acting so childishly.

"You look nice, Nyla, really you do," said Flossie. "Awfully nice."

After a while the Eskimo girl glanced at herself again. When she had got over her first embarrassment at finding herself so changed, she became very much interested in her appearance. She turned this way and that, fingering the belt of the dress and the soft white ribbon at the collar. She even gave a tug at her curls to make sure that it was really her own hair still firmly attached to her head!

"I tell you what," said Flossie, jumping down from her chair, "let's take Nyla's picture as she is now. Would you like that, Nyla?"

The little girl consented to the picture taking, although she was afraid of the white man's camera, as were all the natives. After several snapshots had been taken, the people of the settlement gathered around, speaking about Nyla's changed appearance. The Eskimo girl began to giggle again and put her hands before her face.

Anuk seemed very well pleased with the way his daughter looked. "She like white girl now," he grunted. "Very nice. Very good."

Meanwhile, Bert had won Puk's gratitude by teaching the lad to make a small model ship. Bert was very good at this sort of work. Every detail was thought out carefully.

Puk sat beside the white boy as Bert carved little smoke-stacks for the ship and cut out tiny windows in the cabin. The Eskimo was very happy when Bert let him help with these tasks and pleased when the Bobbsey lad would ask his advice about something that had to do with building the ship.

All this time there came no word from Mr. Bobbsey. Once in a while men would arrive at the settlement and pass through it on their way to Hudson Bay. Some of them were trappers, but only a few had been as far inland as White Hope. Those who had, however, said the snow was very deep in that part of the country, and that most of the trails were almost impossible to follow.

Bert had put to good use the Eskimo words he had learned, for he spoke to a number of trappers in their own language, regarding his father.

"I'm proud of you," praised his mother. "You are a great help to me."

"I have one idea about getting word to Daddy, but I'm keeping it a secret until a certain time," the boy explained.

"Really?" said Mrs. Bobbsey. "That's interesting."

Freddie entered at that moment. "I have an idea, too."

"Yes?" asked his mother, smiling a bit.

"I bet Daddy's up with Santa Claus at the North Pole."

One day, when Anuk was bound for the docks to meet an incoming steamer laden with supplies for the settlement, the twins begged so hard to go along that Anuk finally said they might. It was decided that Nyla and Puk should accompany them. It was lots of

fun mushing across the snow, with Palla fully re-
covered and once more leading the husky-team.

At the waterfront they found that the ship had just
arrived. The twins, with Anuk, Puk and Nyla, went
aboard. While Anuk attended to his business, the
captain, a pleasant person with a real genuine liking
for all the young people, took the children about his
boat.

If Bert and Puk had only stayed with the group
they would have been all right. But Bert wanted to
see the engine-room, and Puk, who had listened with
wide-eyed interest to the white boy's wonderful
stories of machinery and how it was made to run, was
equally eager.

The lads made the rounds of the engine-room and
were on their way back to the deck, when Bert was
surprised to hear below them the throb of motors.

The ship was moving!

CHAPTER XX

BERT and Puk rushed up to the deck, but they were too late. The gulf of ice-choked water between them and land was already very wide. It grew more so as they watched it.

"I'll find the captain," cried Bert. "Maybe he can still put us ashore."

However, the captain said it was too late. His boat was already behind schedule. The boys would have to go on to the next stop where they could catch a steamer back to Cold Star.

"I guess we're in for it," said Bert, coming back to Puk. "The captain says we will have to go on to Frozen Bridge and take the boat back from there."

The passengers were very nice to the two stranded lads. A pleasant old man, travelling with his son, looked after them very carefully. He was a determined old gentleman, and asked the boys many questions, mostly about Cold Star settlement and Miss Lamson's work there. He even took them to his state-room where he called the steward and had him bring sandwiches and milk, with a big slice of chocolate cake for each of them.

In this way Bert and Puk passed the time until they

147

got to Frozen Bridge. They had been treated so
kindly that they were rather sorry to leave the old
man and other acquaintances aboard the warm and
comfortable steamer. It had been a nice change from
all the cold and frozen country they had seen for so
long.

Frozen Bridge was only a group of old buildings
with a general store to supply the needs of the few
people who lived there. The front of the shop was
filled with furs. Pelts of all kinds lay on the counter
and hung from the rafters of the rude roof.

Two trappers were in the place, one of them an
old Eskimo, the other a tall, hulking white man who
was the owner. One of them had unstrapped a big
bundle of pelts and was arguing about their price.
The other was talking to the Eskimo.

No one appeared to notice the lads as they entered
the store. "Nice place," grinned Puk, opening the
door.

Bert went over to the stove in the centre of the
room and held out his hands to the welcome heat. He
was about to speak to Puk, when something about the
old Eskimo caught his eye. He looked more closely at
the man. No, he had not been mistaken. The old
Eskimo was Looktoo, the medicine-man!

Bert knew that Looktoo had been driven from his
native village by his own people, who no longer had
any faith in his power to cure them of their ills. He
had heard that the old fellow had disappeared and
that no one knew where he had gone. To find him
here in Frozen Bridge was a great surprise to Bert.
He moved a little closer to the counter, and beckoned
to Puk to follow him.

The medicine-man had his back to the two boys. Bert heard him grunt at one of the trappers and say, "You come from place call White Hope?"

The man shrugged and answered in fairly good English, "My frien', no one come from White Hope. It is bury deep in snow, that one. Heaviest snow in ten, maybe twelve, year. All through there it is same. High drifts, no trails, no nothing."

"Maybe you meet white man—big white man. He smile all time," questioned Looktoo.

"This white man, he have a name, I suppose?" returned the trapper with a good-natured grin.

"They call him—Bobbsey," said Looktoo. "One other white man be with him. You see him, yes?"

The trapper shook his head. It was evident that he was losing interest in the conversation.

"I tell you I see no one, my frien'. This man Bobbsey," he added, and you may be sure Bert was listening with both his ears, "he live at White Hope, yes?"

At this point Puk tugged at Bert's arm to tell him that the steamer had arrived. In turning a second to answer his friend, Bert almost missed hearing the Eskimo's reply.

He caught the word "Lenland", however, and some more conversation, from which he found out that his father was staying at that place. He did not dare to wait any longer and question the Eskimo, much as he wanted to, for fear of missing the return boat to Cold Star.

"Do you know where Lenland is?" Bert asked of Puk as they hurried up the gangplank.

Puk shrugged, but made no other reply. After a moment he said a trifle sadly, "Lenland far away. Far away in back country."

This information was not enough to suit Bert. As soon as they got on the boat he sought out the captain and repeated to him the question he had put to Puk.

"Lenland?" said the captain. "Why yes, I have heard of it. A post has been established there, I believe, with a small population; very few whites, most of them Eskimos and Indians. Not thinking of going there, I hope?" he added.

"No—at least, I'm afraid they won't let me go," said Bert. He paused, then looked at the captain, his glance very direct and serious. "I wish you would tell me, Captain, just what the chances are of getting a dogsled through to Lenland."

The skipper looked serious. "Not much chance, I'm afraid, son," he said. "Lenland is hard enough to get to at any time. But just now, with the unusually heavy, early snows, I doubt if anyone could get through."

As he noticed Bert's downcast face the captain added kindly, "But why do you ask, son? Is there any reason why you want to get through to Lenland right now?"

"I have just heard that my father is near there," Bert said. He added desperately, "We will have to find some way to get through to him. I don't know how, but we'll do it."

The captain shook his head. He sympathized deeply with Bert, but realized how impossible it would be for the lad to reach his father.

"Sorry, son," he said. "Wish you luck, anyway."

"Thanks," said Bert.

During the rest of that return trip to Cold Star the Bobbsey boy felt very sad. Even the wonderful greeting of the twins at the landing-stage did very little to cheer him up. All the lad could think of was his mother, and how he would go about breaking this news to her.

It was after dark when Puk and Bert reached the settlement. Lamps were burning in the main room, and the light from them made flickering patches on the ground outside the windows.

The dogs began barking as the boys arrived, while children started shouting. Doors burst open, and people poured out to greet the returning sled.

Mrs. Bobbsey hugged the twins, she was so happy, and she even kissed Puk and Nyla in her delight at having them all safe home again. It was when she saw Bert's face in the pale light from one of the windows that she knew something was bothering him.

"Bert, you have bad news!" she cried. "What is it?"

CHAPTER XXI

A DARING PILOT

IN the big room, warm and bright with firelight, Bert told his story.

"Father is in Lenland," he said, as he related to his mother how he had heard Looktoo talking to a man at Frozen Bridge. "Of course, the trapper may be wrong, but he seemed very sure of what he was saying. And if Dad is in or near Lenland, there is no way of our getting through to him."

"But what makes you so sure of that?" Mrs. Bobbsey asked anxiously.

Bert told her of the conversation he had had with the steamer captain. Mrs. Bobbsey refused to accept that man's opinion as final. She called in Miss Lamson and Doctor Bramley, and asked them about it. The two settlement workers were forced to agree with the captain, although they disliked having to cause Mrs. Bobbsey any worry.

"I am afraid he is right," said Miss Lamson. "Lenland is so very far in the interior that it is dangerous to try to journey there even under the most favourable conditions. It would be almost sure death for anyone to try to do so now."

"But there must be someone who would be willing

to make the attempt," said Mrs. Bobbsey. She looked pleadingly at Doctor Bramley. "Suppose Richard has become ill from exposure. He has never been in such a place before. Surely I can find someone who will be able to reach him—at least try," she finished pitifully.

Dr. Bramley paused. A look of deep understanding passed between him and Miss Lamson. Then he turned to Mrs. Bobbsey, his kindly face troubled and sad.

"I should be in error, were I to encourage you, Mrs. Bobbsey," he said. "I am afraid you could find no one at Cold Star, nor at any of the neighbouring villages, who would be willing to attempt a journey to Lenland at this time of year. I am afraid you will have to be patient—and wait."

"Meanwhile, what of Richard?" cried poor Mrs. Bobbsey. "He may be sick. He may even die. Does no one care about that?"

"I do, Mother," said Flossie, half sobbing.

"And so do I," said Freddie sturdily.

Mrs. Bobbsey drew the small twins close to her.

"Don't cry, Mother. Please don't cry," said Flossie, looking for her handkerchief.

Bert went over and put his arms about his mother, wishing that he might be able to think of something to say to comfort her. Mrs. Bobbsey looked up at her "big boy", and smiled through her tears.

"We will find someone to go, won't we, Bert?" she said.

Bert cleared his throat before he answered.

"Sure we will, Mother," he said. "Don't you worry, we'll find someone, all right."

This, however, proved to be much easier to think about than actually to carry out. The next morning

Mrs. Bobbsey, in a far more hopeful mood, went from house to house in the settlement and nearby villages, trying to find someone who would be willing to brave danger and undertake the trip to Lenland.

Poor Mrs. Bobbsey had no success whatever. The mention of the name Lenland was enough to cause the natives to tremble with fear and awe. They said they would have nothing to do with the place, nor would they consider any proposition which might be offered them if they would undertake such a perilous journey at this time of year. Mrs. Bobbsey, together with Bert and Puk, who had accompanied her, were finally forced to give up the attempt and return to the settlement.

In the meantime, the small twins had remained there with Nan. Freddie and Flossie were so saddened by the mother's worry and by their own anxiety over the long absence of Daddy Bobbsey, that Nan found it necessary to hide her own feelings in an effort to amuse the twins, and bring back to them their usual sunny spirits.

"Let's have a snowball fight," she proposed. "Some fresh snow fell last night, you know, so we shouldn't find it any trouble at all to make a fort and a lot of ammunition. What do you say?"

"I say 'yes'," said Freddie. "But I want you on my side, Nan," he added.

"Well, I don't mind having Nyla," stated Flossie. "She makes nice big snowballs, and can throw straight, too."

The children put on boots and fur parkas, tying the hoods snugly under their chins. Soon they were busily engaged in piling the snow into a high ridge to make their fort. Nyla and Flossie were on one side, Nan and Freddie on the other, and they rolled and patted handfuls of snow into huge balls of ammunition.

Suddenly Freddie raised his head and sent a shot over the ridge. Flossie ducked, and the ball caught her right on top of her fur hood.

"Hi, got you that time," yelled her brother. "Why don't you fight back? Why don't you?"

For answer a shower of shot and shell broke from Flossie and Nyla's side of the fort. Nan and Freddie instantly answered with a volley of ammunition. The battle was on!

For several minutes the air was filled with snowballs smashed in mid-air, and particles of ice broken off from them and falling like a shower of sleet. The children shouted and furiously made more ammunition. It was plain to be seen that neither side would be caught napping!

At the height of the battle, the far-away rumbling of an aeroplane was heard. At first it sounded so soft that the children scarcely noticed it. Then nearer and nearer it came, until the roar of motors suddenly seemed to fill the air, drowning out all other sounds.

The children stopped their play to look up into the sky. People began running out of the settlement buildings.

"It's a plane!" shouted Freddie. A great big plane!"

Mrs. Bobbsey had just returned with Bert and Puk from her unsuccessful search to find someone to look for Mr. Bobbsey, and were just in time to see the big monoplane make a perfect landing on the broad ice-field outside the settlement.

By the time the pilot had climbed down from his cockpit a crowd had gathered about him.

The aviator, bundled up to his eyes in fur, waved an arm in greeting. His glance fell on Bert, who had come up with Mrs. Bobbsey, and was standing close to the plane.

"Hi, young fellow," he said pleasantly, "will you keep an eye on my plane while I go to the settlement and have a word with Miss Lamson? These folks," with a wave of his hand towards the crowding natives, love to hack out pieces of my plane to keep as souvenirs."

"Sure, I'll take care of it for you, Mr. Faber," said Bert.

The pilot looked at him sharply.

"So you know me, eh?" he asked.

"Yes, sir," Bert replied. "I was there the time your plane crashed into the tree. Do you remember?"

"Oh, yes, I remember," said Alfred Faber with a smile. "That's one of the things a pilot doesn't forget, young fellow. Well, look after the bus, will you? Much obliged."

Bert took his responsibility in this regard very seriously. He was delighted to think that a pilot as experienced as Mr. Faber was had so much faith in him. Bert warned back the natives in such a way that it sounded as if he were the owner of the plane instead of Mr. Faber.

Meanwhile, the pilot had walked rapidly across

the frozen ground to the settlement. He found Miss Lamson working in one of the rooms in the main building.

"Well, I've come through safely, Helen," said the young man with his pleasing grin. "Aren't you glad to see me?"

"You have been away so long, Alfred," said the teacher, tears of happiness in her eyes. "I began to think something dreadful must have happened to you. Why has it taken you so much time to get here?"

"That's a long story. But before going into it," the pilot said firmly, "there is a question I should like to ask you. When will you marry me?"

Miss Lamson dried her eyes and smiled at him.

"I haven't said I would at all yet, you know," she reminded him.

Before Al Faber could say anything further, which he seemed very eager to do, he was attracted to the window by the sound of a sharp scuffle outside.

"I believe those natives are at my plane," he said with a frown. "I'll have to go, Helen. But," he paused at the door to smile at her, "I'll be back, so wait for me."

At the plane Faber found Bert and Puk in a fight with two Eskimo lads from a neighbouring village. Bert, aided by Puk, was winning when the pilot walked into the midst of flailing arms and fists.

"Here, here" cried the aviator. "What's wrong? Trying to kill each other, are you?"

"The other kids wanted to climb aboard your plane," Freddie explained. "Bert and Puk wouldn't let them."

"Good work," said Al Faber with a nod of approval. "Thanks a lot, boys. Maybe I can do something for you some day."

The words were spoken carelessly, but to Bert they sounded very exciting.

"You *can* do a real favour for me, Mr. Faber," said the lad earnestly. "You can help me find my father!"

CHAPTER XXII

A DANGEROUS SEARCH

ALFRED FABER looked surprised. "Your father?" he repeated. "Lost, eh? Where?"

"Near a place called Lenland," Freddie said importantly.

"We are afraid he's sick and needs help," Flossie added. "You will go to look for our daddy, won't you, Mr. Pilot?"

Flossie's lips trembled, and two big tears stood in her blue eyes. The man turned his gaze from her to Freddie's small figure and then to Bert, who stood by waiting anxiously for his answer.

"Well, now this will bear looking into," said the young man with a slow smile. "Suppose we all go inside the house where it's warm and comfortable while you tell me your story. How would that be?"

The twins agreed that that would be very nice indeed. They waited patiently while the pilot made his plane safe; then they all went with him to the largest settlement building. There the little group was joined by Nan, Mrs. Bobbsey and Miss Lamson. The small twins ran over to their mother and drew her into a chair.

"Mother, Mr. Faber is going to find Daddy," Freddie cried.

"Well, he didn't exactly say so," Flossie added seriously. "But he did say he'd think about it. And I believe he really will go. Won't you, Mr. Faber?"

"Flossie, Freddie, I don't know what to say," exclaimed Mrs. Bobbsey. She looked anxiously at the pilot. "I am afraid the trip to Lenland would be a very dangerous one, even in a plane. I can't ask you to undertake such a risk for—someone who can mean nothing to you."

"But that's just where you are wrong, Mrs. Bobbsey," said the pilot quickly. "Your husband does mean something to me. Out here in the great North country all men are brothers. We must get together and fight off the danger of death from storm and famine. The snows, the thaws, in fact, all the dangers we meet here are our enemies. We have to help one another."

"I have been trying all morning to find someone who might be willing to try to get a team through to my husband," said Mrs. Bobbsey. "None of the people I interviewed have your kind and helpful spirit, Mr. Faber. I found not a single person who would even so much as promise to make the trip. Bert has a secret idea for getting news through. What is it, son?"

"I remembered that Mr. Faber said he was coming up here, and I thought if he should he might make a search for Daddy," answered Bert simply, "by plane."

"Would it be safe, Al?" Miss Lamson asked quietly.

Faber turned the question aside with a shrug of his shoulders, and smiled at her.

"Safe enough for me to try it, Helen. And now," he said, turning to Mrs. Bobbsey, "how about this trip? When would you like me to start?"

Flossie and Freddie flung themselves upon the young man, fairly strangling him with joy and thanks.

"Oh, then you will go to find our daddy!" they cried.

"I knew you would," Freddie added.

The thanks of Mrs. Bobbsey and the older twins, though not as noisy as those of Freddie and Flossie, were every bit as sincere.

With Nan to help her, Mrs. Bobbsey prepared a box of supplies to be taken to her husband. It contained only the things he needed most, for the pilot had told her that the lighter the plane the better would be his chance of making the trip without any trouble.

The twins were very busy. Nan and Bert wrote long letters to their father, in which they told him how much they had missed him, and how they longed for him to come back again.

Nan was just about to seal hers, when Flossie came up, holding a pair of scissors in her hand.

"Goodness, what are you going to do with those?" cried Nan. "Do be careful, Flossie. You might cut yourself."

"I don't want to cut *myself*. I want to cut off a piece of my hair," Flossie announced.

"What for?"

"To send to Daddy," returned the little girl. "I

think it would be better than for me to write a letter to him. I have to print all the words, you know, and it takes so long. So I think I'll send Daddy a little curl instead."

Nan hugged her sister.

"What a good idea," she cried. "I'll cut off a little bit of your hair right here in the back, where it won't show. Do be careful, Flossie," she added, as the girl gave an excited jump. "If you wiggle like that I may stick the scissors right into you."

"I can't help it when I think of Daddy maybe coming home," Flossie explained. "I get so happy, I just can't help it."

Nan tied a blue ribbon about the lock of fair hair which, until recently, had grown on Flossie's head. Flossie tucked it, ribbon and all, into an envelope. On the outside she printed in big, painstaking letters:

TO DADDY
WITH LOVE
FROM FLOSSIE

Freddie had been watching Flossie, and it made him feel like sending his daddy something, too. The little boy thought at first that he might give Daddy Bobbsey some of *his* hair, but when he thought it over there seemed to be several objections to this. In the first place, his hair was so short it would be hard to cut off a really good-sized lock of it. Then, too, he felt that it would be sort of silly to send a piece of his hair in a letter, even to Daddy. It was the sort of thing girls did, but boys never would.

For a long time the little lad sat there thinking very hard. Suddenly his face brightened.

"I know what I'll do," he thought. "I'll send Daddy my fire-engine. He'll guess who did it, all right, and it'll be lots better than an old lock of hair. Golly, I'm glad I thought of it!"

Early the next morning everybody in the settlement was up. Excitement was in the air as they ate their breakfasts in a big hurry and followed Al Faber out to his plane.

The aviator and Miss Lamson managed to have a few words together before the others came up.

"You will be careful, won't you, Al?" the teacher asked anxiously. "Please don't take any unnecessary risks. Promise?"

"Not one," the pilot answered cheerfully. He suddenly smiled at her. "I have a special reason for wanting to get back safe—and soon," he reminded her. "You still owe me the answer to a certain question."

The others came up just then and immediately all was in confusion. The twins were full of last-minute messages they were very eager for Al Faber to give to their daddy from them.

The young man answered that he would tell Mr. Bobbsey all of them he could remember. He had gone over the plane thoroughly to make sure that everything was in readiness for the take-off.

Now he stepped back with a cry of annoyance. He held in his hand a thick, bulky parcel wrapped in newspapers.

"This can't go. It's too heavy. Great Scott!" he

cried, uncovering the bulky object, "it's a fire-engine!"

"I wanted to send it to Daddy," Freddie explained, feeling highly embarrassed.

"Sorry, young fellow, but I'm afraid you will have to send your father something that isn't so heavy," said the airman kindly. "I won't be able to take your fire-engine with me."

Freddie's feelings were deeply hurt. He knew that if the plane were to go off without his toy there would be no message on it at all from him to his daddy. The little boy could not bear to think of that.

He chose a moment when no one was paying any attention to him, and quietly climbed into the cockpit of the plane. There he crouched down, making himself just as small as he possibly could.

He wondered if anyone had seen him. His heart beat so hard he was sure everyone near the aircraft could hear it!

CHAPTER XXIII

THE SECRET IN THE STONE HUT

NO one had seen Freddie enter the plane; and of course no one could hear his heart beating, loud as it sounded to Freddie. In fact, he was as near as possible to doing what he wanted to, when something occurred.

Al Faber had climbed into his seat. He was fastening the strap of his helmet when Freddie, shaking all over with excitement, heard Nan say, "Has anyone seen Freddie? He was right here a moment ago."

The little boy held his breath and crouched still lower in his hiding-place. He wished Al Faber would hurry and take-off before anyone thought of looking in the plane.

For an exciting moment it seemed as if Freddie's wish might come true. He heard the pilot call good-bye to someone. Then the roar of the engine sounded loud in the little boy's ears.

"Now we're going to start," thought Freddie, feeling very happy, though just the least bit frightened. "We are going straight up into the air!"

"Wait a minute! Oh, wait a minute, Mr. Faber," called a voice which Freddie recognized as that of his mother. "We can't find my little boy anywhere. Are you sure he isn't in the plane with you?"

The noise of the motor was suddenly choked off. Freddie's heart was in his mouth. He knew the game was up. They would search the plane now, and of course they would find him. He sighed and stood up.

"I wanted to go to Lenland to see Daddy," he explained to his relieved though slightly upset family. "Now I suppose I can't."

"Freddie Bobbsey, come down out of that plane at once!" cried his mother.

She was too glad to find her little boy safe to scold him very much. She only held his hand in her own more tightly than usual, while the machine encircled the field, gathering speed for the take-off.

Al Faber waved to them and they waved back, shouting:

"Good-bye! Good luck! Come back to us soon!"

They watched the plane until it was only a small dot in the clear, frosty blue of the sky.

"Do you think Mr. Faber will find Daddy, Mother?" Freddie asked.

"Yes," said Mrs. Bobbsey steadily. "He will, I am sure he will!"

Later that morning Puk and Nyla asked the twins if they would like to go for a sled ride to a neighbouring settlement at Deerhead. Anuk, said Puk, would let them take the dogsled.

Of course, the children were delighted with the invitation. Twenty minutes later found them ready for the trip, bundled up to their eyes in furs, and eagerly looking forward to the fun they would have.

Off they went, with Puk flourishing the dog lash. The icy wind stung their cheeks and reddened the tips of their noses. The day was bitterly cold but the sun was shining. The children loved the way it glistened on the ice, making the great plain look like a brilliant jewel.

When they got to Deerhead they left the huskies in the care of a friendly Eskimo, while they went off on foot to do a little exploring on their own account. Puk carried a spear and an old rifle; Bert was also armed with a spear, though he expected to have little use for a weapon of any kind on their present trip.

Puk kept a sharp lookout for possible game. "Maybe we shoot caribou," he explained. "Much caribou this place. We catch him, take him home. Have big feast."

A few moments later Puk's watchfulness was rewarded. He shouted a sharp warning to the children, bidding them lie down and keep very still.

"Caribou behind ridge—over there," said the Eskimo lad. "Wind blow our way. He no smells us. Pretty soon he come out. You watch."

Bert and Freddie did exactly as Puk told them to, but Nan and Flossie felt so sorry for the dumb animal that they would not look, but turned their eyes the other way.

"That wicked Puk," Flossie whispered, half crying. "It's cruel to want to hurt the poor thing. I hope he misses! I hope he does!"

When the shot rang out a moment later, followed almost immediately by the Eskimo boy's shout of joy, Flossie burst into tears and hid her face against Nan's shoulder.

"I think it's horrid," sobbed the little girl. "The poor beast! I want to go home, Nan. Please take me home!"

Nan comforted her little sister as well as she could. She tried to tell her why Puk shot the caribou, pointing out that the natives have to hunt and kill for food in order to keep from starving to death.

Flossie finally stopped crying. On one point she was determined, however. She would not go near the dead caribou.

The small girl's mind was taken off the subject, for Nyla had a suggestion about something else to do. "I know stone hut not far from here," she said. "Natives say white man live there one time. We go see?"

Nan agreed, for she was ever on the lookout for a clue to Harry Weller. She called to Bert, telling him where they were going and that they would soon return. Then, with Flossie's hand clasped tightly in her own, she followed Nyla.

After a long walk over ice that had been frozen in mounds and lumpy, jagged ridges, the girls finally came to the unused hut.

Someone had tried to choke up the entrance with stones. These the girls pulled away, even Flossie helping. It was not long before they had cleared out a space large enough for them to get in by crawling on their hands and knees.

For the first time Flossie hung back, a frightened look in her eyes.

"Suppose there's a bear in there," she whispered. "It looks like a bear cave to me."

"Silly! It isn't a cave at all," laughed Nan. "It's a stone hut. And how in the world do you suppose a bear would ever get in there over all those stones we just cleared away?"

"I don't know," said Flossie thoughtfully. "Maybe it couldn't."

"Of course it couldn't. Look," Nan pointed out, "Nyla has gone inside already. I'll follow her, and if everything is all right you come after me."

Flossie seemed to think this was a very good idea. When Nan called to her from within that there was nothing dangerous in the hut, and that Nyla had even found an old candle and lighted it, Flossie crawled in after the older girls.

The place was nearly bare. What was left of a mixture of rugs lay on the floor. There was a box which had once served as a table, and a three-legged stool that had been used as a chair. Old tins were scattered about, and there were the remains of a long-dead fire on a hearth at one end of the hut.

These things the girls saw by the light of the piece of tallow candle Nyla had found. In examining the hearth, Nan noticed that one of the stones had come loose. Hastily she pulled at it. As she did so, it rolled aside, and she saw in a hollow behind it an old note-book and a piece of paper covered with soot.

"I wonder if these will be a clue to who lived here," she said hopefully.

The piece of paper was a map of some kind. Its lines and markings meant nothing to Nan and she put it down with a puzzled frown.

The notebook was more helpful. On the fly-leaf was a name, under which was a date, both written in a shaky hand. Nan held it close to the candle-light.

"Harry Weller," she read, then paused in her pleasure at finding the clue. "That's the name of the man Daddy has been looking for!"

"White man live here one time," Nyla pointed out to her. "Maybe him Harry Weller."

"Maybe. Anyway, I'm going to keep this note-book and the map. It may be a help to Daddy. I must tell Bert."

There was nothing more to be found in the hut. After one final look around to make sure of this, the girls put out the candle, then, leaving the hut, they returned to the place where they had left the boys.

There they found Bert and Flossie waiting for them alone. Puk, Bert explained, had gone on ahead. He had found an Eskimo who was willing to help him haul the carcass of the caribou to the settlement.

"Puk said he would have the dogs out and the sled waiting for us by the time we reach Deerhead," Bert added. "We'd better hurry. Puk seemed in a big rush to start for home."

On the way to Deerhead Nan showed her brother the map and the notebook she had found in the stone hut. Bert was very much interested. He urged his sister to take care of the papers in the hope that they might be of use to their father later on.

At Deerhead Puk was ready with the sled and dogs. "It get late," said the lad, flourishing his whip. "We hurry."

On the way back they overtook an Eskimo trudging wearily through the snow. Puk pulled up the dogs, intending to offer the man a lift.

The fellow turned sharply, and they saw his face. It was that of Nogasak!

CHAPTER XXIV

BERT BOBBSEY had not seen the bad Eskimo since the day he had disappeared so mysteriously with his dogs from Cold Star settlement. At that time Nogasak had seemed fairly well off. He had been warmly dressed and had plenty to eat, and drove his own team of huskies. In his pocket there had jingled the "white man's money".

Now he looked entirely different. His clothes were worn, and he looked hungry. His team and sled were gone. Nogasak seemed to be without a thing in the world except his spear and a bundle he carried over one shoulder.

The expression on the Eskimo's face was always unpleasant. As he stood looking at the sled full of children and saw, sticking out from the back of it, the freshly killed carcass of the caribou, his face looked so cruel and cunning that even Puk was frightened by it. The Eskimo lad whipped up the dogs and the sled lurched forward.

At this moment Nogasak dropped his spear and bundle on the ice and leaped towards the sled. He was as quick and active as a wolf. In a moment the lines were in his hand, and he had pulled the dogs to a standstill.

"Get out!" he growled to the frightened children. "You walk. Nogasak ride. Get out, I say!"

He reached into the sled and gripped Flossie's arm. The little girl squealed with alarm and leaned against Nan.

"You leave my sister alone," cried Bert furiously.

With these words he flung himself upon Nogasak, flailing wildly with both fists.

"Puk, help me!" Bert gasped.

Puk now rushed into the fray. The weight of the two lads bore Nogasak backwards over the ice. He lost his footing and fell, clutching and clawing, both boys on top of him.

One of the man's outstretched hands touched the spear near the place where he had fallen. His fingers closed about the handle. The look of cunning grew in his eyes as he struggled to pull himself away from the clinging arms and punching fists of the two lads.

Nan saw the danger and cried out a warning.

"Bert, watch out! The spear!" she shouted.

Bert and Puk now saw Nogasak's purpose. They gripped his spear arm and held on with all their strength. But they knew that he was too strong for them. Sooner or later Nogasak would break their grip. And then——

Puk raised himself on one arm and called, "Palla, Poto—come Palla!"

Nogasak was not afraid of the lads, but he *was* afraid of the dogs. As the huskies rushed to the aid of their young master, their teeth bared, their hackles bristling, Nogasak grew stiff with terror. By a desperate effort he shook off the grip of the boys and struggled to his feet.

Palla leaped just as the man staggered backwards, and caught a corner of Nogasak's jacket in his sharp teeth. The fur ripped as the Eskimo pulled himself free. The wretched fellow took to his heels, staggering and stumbling blindly over the ice, his face twisted with fear.

The dogs, now thoroughly aroused, would have followed, but Puk wound his strong fingers in Palla's harness and held him back.

"No more!" Puk grunted. "Nogasak gone. We go."

"Next time I go out, I'm going to carry a spear, too," said Freddie.

The children were glad to start back to Cold Star, for they had been badly frightened. Puk whipped up the dogs and the sled flew over the frozen ground, never slackening its pace until the settlement buildings were reached.

"I have never been so glad to get home before," said Nan, stepping from the sled.

"And I hope we shall never see that horrid old Nogasak again," added Flossie.

And they never did. The unpleasant Eskimo disappeared completely, and from that time on was never seen nor heard of again in Cold Star.

Now followed an anxious time for the Bobbsey family while they awaited news from Lenland. After several days had passed and no word came, they grew more and more anxious.

One day an Eskimo came through from the Lenland region. He was pale and hollow-eyed, half-starved and half-frozen. He told a terrible tale of hardships and almost unbelievable trials he had experienced, all of which served only to increase Mrs. Bobbsey's worries. The traveller said that he had seen no white men, but only some Indians who were in as bad a state as himself.

After several more anxious days a second Eskimo arrived at the settlement. The man was questioned in the recreation room where most of the people had gathered to hear his story.

After describing the unbelievably bad conditions in Lenland, the man spoke of the terrible situation of three white men whom he had met near that country, but had been unable to help.

"White men caught in ice crevasse. They fall in, no can get out again."

"Wasn't there some way you could help them?" Mrs. Bobbsey questioned anxiously. "Do you mean to say that you came away and left those three men— to die, perhaps?"

The Eskimo shrugged. "Need rope," he said stolidly. "No have rope. No can help white men without rope."

"Oh, this is terrible," cried Mrs. Bobbsey with a pitiful glance around at the anxious, sympathetic circle of faces. "If Richard and the two other men are caught in an ice crevasse, as this Eskimo says, how are they to be seen even from the air?"

"Much better from the air than from the ground," said Doctor Bramley gently.

"We must all have courage," Miss Lamson added. She placed a hand on Mrs. Bobbsey's shoulder and smiled at her. "Al can find your husband, if anybody can."

Just before the Eskimo left camp he brought Mrs. Bobbsey a belt which he said he had found near the crevasse into which the three white men had fallen. It was one belonging to Mr. Bobbsey, and was identified by the initials RWB on the buckle.

There was nothing to do now but wait—and hope. The twins tried to fill in the anxious days by playing with Igloo, who had grown into a lively, clumsy puppy, always tripping over his own feet and stopping to bark at nothing at all in the funniest way imaginable. Sometimes the children would trudge to one of the near-by villages to spend a few hours with their friends, the Eskimos. But, no matter what they did, they could not lose their feeling of sadness.

One morning, to cheer them up, Anuk suggested that they all go with him to the steamer dock to get supplies. The twins agreed to this. They felt that anything would be better than moping about the house and thinking all the time of the awful things that might have happened to Daddy Bobbsey.

When they arrived at the place, Anuk went on to a store. The twins, left alone for the time being, wandered down to the water's edge.

"I wish we could go home to Lakeport," said Freddie. His lower lip stuck out the way it sometimes did when he was fighting back tears. "It's too cold here. I want to go home."

"I guess we all do," said Bert gloomily. "We've been away a long time."

"But we can't go home without Daddy," said Flossie, beginning to cry. "Nan, isn't Daddy ever coming back to us?"

"Sh! Of course he is. Don't cry, honey. Oh, look! Up there!"

Above their heads, far up in the sky, Nan saw a speck, a speck that grew steadily larger and larger as she watched it. Wasn't it an aeroplane?

CHAPTER XXV

THE WANDERERS RETURN

"AN aeroplane!" shouted Freddie. "Look, it *is*! Golly, do you think Daddy can be in it?"

The children anxiously watched the plane, their eyes straining to catch a glimpse of their beloved daddy. Would he be on board?

Although they asked themselves the question over and over again, they did not dare to hope too much. They had been disappointed so many times before. Moreover, why should the plane be landing here instead of at Cold Star?

As the aircraft came nearer, a crowd of natives and whites gathered to watch it. Everyone was wondering if it would land there, or go on to some other settlement farther down the Bay.

Excitement grew as it began to come down.

The craft made a perfect landing.

After what seemed like a never-ending wait to the twins, the pilot climbed out of the plane, and turned to assist his passengers.

"That's Alfred Faber, sure," said Bert excitedly. "And there's somebody with him."

"It's Daddy!" cried Freddie with a shout. "Daddy, Daddy, don't you see us? Hi, Daddy!"

The man who had just climbed out of the cockpit and who now stood clinging to the plane, raised his hand and waved to them.

"It *is* Daddy!" sobbed Flossie. "Oh, Nan, Daddy's come back. Daddy's come *back*!"

Never before had those bleak shores seen such a reunion as that one! Mr. Bobbsey, greatly changed, and very thin and weak from illness and lack of food, clasped his children to him as though he would never let them go again.

He patted Flossie's cheek and called her his "little fat fairy". He gripped Bert's shoulders and pulled Freddie's nose—which was very red with the cold and his effort to keep back the tears of joy. He had a special smile and word of cheer for Nan, his "big girl".

A second sled was hired from an Eskimo at the dock since Anuk's sled, loaded down as it was with provisions, was not nearly large enough to carry them all. The children were told that the plane was out of fuel, and could not go on to Cold Star.

It was not until they were on their way back to the settlement that the twins found out who Al Faber's second passenger was. He was Harry Weller, the man for whose sake Mr. Bobbsey had risked his own life, and who had caused the lumberman's family to spend many long weeks of worry and anxiety.

After dinner that night the twins heard the full story of Mr. Bobbsey's adventures. They were all seated in the big recreation room. Mr. Bobbsey, Al Faber, and Mr. Harry Weller had places of honour on the large sofa. Flossie and Freddie, with Igloo between them, sprawled comfortably on a bearskin rug in front of the fire. Nan had brought up a foot-stool to sit on, while Bert was astride a chair, watching his father steadily.

Mrs. Bobbsey smiled upon them all, but her gaze wandered most often to Mr. Bobbsey. It was easy to tell, just by looking at her, how happy she was to have her family gathered with her again.

Miss Lamson was there, of course, and Doctor Bramley. Even the red-haired nurse had left her patients for the time being and had come in to sit between the two Miss Talleys.

Mr. Bobbsey began his story by telling of the meeting with Nogasak.

"I had met the trappers, Joslind and Sakey, by that time," said Mr. Bobbsey. "They were bound for White Hope, too, so we decided to throw in our fortunes and go on together."

Then came Nogasak, whose false directions had sent the three white men off on a wild goose chase. While they were still lost, the blizzard overtook them and they were forced to seek shelter with their dogs and the two native runners in a group of deserted, tumbledown sheds.

Mr. Bobbsey went on to tell how the two runners, who had started out with him from Cold Star settlement, had taken one of the sleds and a team of huskies in a desperate attempt to reach a native village where they could get some supplies.

"That was only a few days after the blizzard," Mr. Bobbsey said sadly. "We never heard of the men again.

"By this time we were getting low on supplies, as you can well imagine. We had to put ourselves and the huskies on rations. The dogs, savage from hunger, fell to fighting among themselves. Before we could separate them, several of them were so badly injured we had to shoot them to put them out of their misery."

At this point Mr. Bobbsey faltered and placed a hand over his eyes. Mrs. Bobbsey said gently, "Don't talk any more if it tires you, Richard. We can hear the rest later."

"There isn't much more," said the twins' father, rousing himself. "Things went from bad to worse with us. An Eskimo passed through once, half-dead, his dogs like scarecrows. He promised if he managed to get through alive to send back help to us. None ever came."

"We sent Anuk," Miss Lamson told him. "He couldn't find you. He came back, after a while, half-starved and nearly frozen to death."

Mr. Bobbsey nodded. "Later we started out again, hoping to reach Lenland, which Sakey and Joslind said was somewhere near," he continued. "The going was hard. One day, when we were trying to climb an icy cliff, we slipped and fell into a deep crevasse from which there was no means of escape. We might have been there yet," he added with a grateful smile at Al Faber, "if it had not been for the timely arrival of our friend here.

"He found us, and took us on to Lenland where luck at last began to smile on me. I found Mr. Weller."

"For which I shall be grateful until I die," said the tall, thin man with the pleasant smile whom the children had come to know as Harry Weller. "I don't see how I can ever thank you for bringing the word of good fortune to a broken, sick old explorer who never had more than a few cents at one time in his life. Now I can go home and regain my health in peace. I should be happier, however," he added, a frown clouding his thoughtful face, "if I could find a map and a notebook belonging to me that contain notes and information of all the research work I have done in recent years; wasted years, if my book is lost."

At the first mention by Mr. Weller of his lost papers Nan had run from the room. Now she returned and held out to the explorer the book and sheet of soot-stained paper which she, Nyla and Flossie had found in the old hut.

"Will these be of any use to you?" she asked.

Mr. Weller took the book and map from her.

"Yes, yes, this is mine," he cried, ruffling the pages of the book with feverish interest. "It contains the result of years of research. Tell me, child, how did you get it?"

Nan explained about the visit to the stone hut. Now that she recalled the place to his mind, the explorer remembered that at one time when he was very sick, he had been cared for by an old Eskimo woman who had hidden his precious papers at his request, later to disappear without telling him where she had placed them.

"I had been very ill, and for a while my memory

was not good," Mr. Weller continued. "I could not remember where I had left my book and map. How can I thank you for finding them for me!"

Nan replied that she deserved no thanks, but was very glad to have been of service to her father's friend.

Here Bert interrupted to ask what had become of the trappers, Sakey and Joslind.

"They went on with Mr. Faber and myself to Lenland," Mr. Bobbsey explained, "where they obtained a sled and fresh supplies. They will mush in as soon as the weather permits, hunting and trapping as they go. Fine fellows, Sakey and Joslind," he added. "Plucky and courageous, good comrades in an emergency. I'd like to see them again, but of course the chances are I never shall."

"And now we can go back home, can't we, Daddy?" said Flossie, climbing on her father's knee. "There isn't anything to keep us here any longer, is there?"

"Not a thing," said Mr. Bobbsey. Over the little girl's head he caught Mrs. Bobbsey's eye. "We will start home," he said, "whenever you like."

"That's good," cried Freddie from the hearth-rug. "Let's go tomorrow, Daddy. Shall we?"

Several days later the Bobbsey family stood on the deck of the steamer which was to take them on the first part of their journey home.

They had said good-bye to Anuk, Puk, Nyla, and all their other good friends at the settlement. Soon they were to make new friends in a very different and exciting way. It is told in "The Bobbsey Twins in

Echo Valley". But just now they were interested only in the boat trip.

Freddie looked at Miss Lamson and Alfred Faber, who were standing close together at the rail.

"Why are they going back with us, Nan?"

"Because they are to be married," his sister replied. "They want to be married in the States."

"I'm glad I'm from the United States and I'm glad I'm going home," said Flossie. "Aren't you, Freddie?"

"Sure I am!" said the little boy sturdily.

A whistle blew with a sharp blast as the steamer moved slowly away from shore. Once more the Bobbsey twins were bound for Lakeport.

Read more of the Twins' adventures in
"THE BOBBSEY TWINS ON THE PONY TRAIL"